R01 0270 2⁴

P9-AOZ-112

Life, Wonderful Life!

By the same author

MY DARLING FROM THE LIONS

BIRTH OF AN OLD LADY

CHARADE

THREE WHO LOVED

ECHO IN ASIA

THE TOIL AND THE DEED

THE FLOWERS OF HIROSHIMA

THE SEEDS OF HIROSHIMA

LOVE TO VIETNAM

THE SOLD DANCER

LIFE, Wonderful LIFE!

Edita Morris

George Braziller

NEW YORK

Copyright © 1971 by Edita Morris
Published simultaneously in Canada by Doubleday Canada, Limited.
All rights reserved.

For information, address the publisher:
George Braziller, Inc.
One Park Avenue, New York 10016

Standard Book Number: 0–8076–0614–6
Library of Congress Catalog Card Number: 73–156598

First printing

Printed in the United States of America

DESIGNED AT THE INKWELL STUDIO

71A   22643

FOR IVAN

AUTHOR'S NOTE

My first novel, *My Darling from the Lions,* was published by Atlantic-Little, Brown in 1943, went into some six printings, and was subsequently acquired by The Viking Press. Pascal Covici, my editor at Viking, was of the opinion that the second part of the novel was not a proper sequel to the first part, and that the first part should be published as a complete work in itself. Good friend and good editor, Pat was quite right, and indeed he had such a project in mind, but his death cancelled its execution. It is only now, when a new reading public has come of age, that thanks to George Braziller, my present publisher, Pat's wish and mine has been fulfilled. I have revised the original text where it seemed advisable, added a few sections to round out the whole, and called the new work *Life, Wonderful Life!* for that is what it means to me, an evocation and a celebration.

E. M.

Paris, 1971

Life, Wonderful Life!

I

Jezza's Story

"Beautiful, beautiful sister-in-law," Uncle Rolf said to Aunt Ninna at breakfast, "may I suggest that you hold your dressing gown together? Not that I think much of modesty as a virtue, to tell the truth." Aunt Ninna didn't move a finger. She was almost asleep, and her lovely hair fell down her shoulders onto the tablecloth. "Ninna is always coming apart," Aunt Emilia said. "She's either asleep or about to go to sleep." She dug her spoon into her egg so hard that the yellow squirted over the table, and she kept glaring at Auntie Ninna. "You may not like it," she said, "but I've decided not to take you to town to help with the Christmas shopping. I'm fed up with you, Ninna. I'll take one of the children instead. I'll take Jezza." She had her mouth full of bread and honey and was eating in the way they tell us not to eat. They tell us to watch Aunt Emilia and see how aw-

ful it looks when she eats. Because of all that breakfast in her mouth it was hard to hear her, but Auntie
Ninna woke up right away. She didn't say anything.
She took one look at Aunt Emilia with her mouth
loaded, and then she walked out of the dining room,
not holding her dressing gown together at all. I
knew she had been aching to get off to town, and that
now she was going back to sleep the whole day, because there is nothing else for her to do up here in
Berg. I felt Anna's legs squeezing mine beneath the
table, and I squeezed hers back for answer. As soon
as we could, we got up and ran to the staircase that
is never used and where we can be alone. Anna said,
"She didn't talk about my going to town too, did
she? I didn't know we could be separated. I never
thought of it as something that might really happen." "We must do something about it," I said. "I
must find a word that will explain to everyone, even
to awful Aunt Emilia, why two people who belong
together never can be separated. There is such a
word. There is the right word for every single thing,
if only one knows first just how one feels about every
single thing. That's why I'll be a writer one day,
because I know how to feel and then I know how to
say how I feel. I'm going to think of that word, and
then they'll let Aunt Ninna go to town instead of me,
and she can wear her big hat with the feathers and
all the men will run after her with their tongues
hanging out as Aunt Emilia says they do. And that'll
be a good thing, because when one has bad lungs as

Auntie Ninna does, one needs lots of fun. If you just leave me for two minutes, I'll think of that big word that says two people who love each other shouldn't ever have to be apart."

2

Anna's Story

I knew it had snowed. I knew it. That was yesterday, the day Aunt Emilia told Jezza that she was going to take her to town. I had been saying snow prayers since the first of October, not silly mushy ones like they say in church, but real ones. Like ants praying that no one will step in their ant heap, or prod them the way we sometimes do. Or strawberries praying that the rain will stop when it rains and rains just when it is time for them to get red and big and they have to sit and be small and sour instead. That's the sort of prayers I mean. Before the first of October we can't expect an awful lot of snow, and it seems that in southern Sweden there isn't snow till November. So I began on the first, and on the sixth it came, in the night. After I had woken, I lay and thought without opening my eyes at all. I thought it was night and that I was out in a garden, just standing there. Everything was black and hard and the sky looked achingly cold. It was real misery—not for me, as I knew what was coming, but for the others, the hedgehogs and the mice. Then from heaven came a snowflake, and it landed right on my hand. It melted and became a drop, and then two more fell from heaven, and four more, and many, many, many more. I bent down and looked at the ground, and it was not black and stiff any longer, but white and soft, and there were surprises in it. I mean when a twig lies on the ground, the snow makes much of it. It puts a long dress over it, just the twig's shape. Or when someone has thrown away an old shoe, the shoe gets a whole white house built over it. There were surprises like that everywhere. The water barrel had a white top, the bushes had white tops too, everything had beautiful white tops, and there was a whole new garden. And then I began to think of a warm garden with noisy birds and leaves that blew about and rubbed against each other and with somebody whistling, and I felt how much more I loved the garden that had no sound at all, and the trees that are made of snow, and the winter flowers of ice that grow on our windowpanes up here in the far North. I opened my eyes and looked at the real snow that was stacked on the window sill, and I thought what a fine day I was beginning. The day is something I walk out on every morning, like a long new carpet. As I come nearer to evening, the carpet in front of me gets shorter, and the part behind me longer. I can see my footprints running along it, and other people's footprints crossing it. I hate to see a lot of tracks on my carpet. It is only Jezza's and my tracks I like to see. I got out of bed and I went over to Jezza's bed to say good-morning. I sat down on her. That woke her. I showed her the trees with white tops outside, and she ran over to the window. She wanted to open it and feel the snow on the ledge, because she always wants to put her hands in everything, in snow or water or anything she sees. I never want to do that. It's like breaking things. Anyway, the window was glued fast with ice, so she couldn't open it, and our pitcher also had a round, fine little cake of ice on top. Jezza shouted that she'd have to get a new cord for her sled, because the old one had broken last year, and she'd have to get some sandpaper to get the rust off her skates. She laughed and ran about and was so pleased with the snow, not because it was beautiful but because now she could get on things that moved quickly, sleds and skates and skis, things that moved quick, quick, the way Jezza always loves to move. And it was this fine day that Aunt Emilia had to go and spoil.

3
Jezza's Story

As we were going to Aunt Emilia to tell her not to take me to town, we met Uncle Rolf in the hall. He stood in the sunshine and his teeth shone and the gun on his shoulder shone. He had on his long bearskin coat that everyone makes fun of because it is so enormous. It comes right down to his feet. The tailor in Bo wouldn't make it at first, but afterwards everyone wanted a coat just like it. That's how it always is with Uncle Rolf. People want to do and look and be like him, but they can't, because they aren't so marvelous. He had snow on his bearskin cap, a huge package of snow right on top of the frozen fur. Anna tried to drag me away because she didn't want to tell Uncle Rolf that we were going to Aunt Emilia. Anna never wants to tell anybody anything. She talks hardly at all, except to me, but I took hold of Uncle Rolf and said, "Aunt Emilia said I have to go to town with her, but she didn't say that Anna was coming along. Uncle Rolf, tell her she doesn't understand. Anna and I can't be in two different places." Uncle Rolf didn't look at me, but he stared at Anna as he always does, and said, "Are you sure she didn't ask you, too?" Anna didn't answer, because she never likes to answer. Uncle Rolf smiled and said, "Anna of the silent mouth! Tell me now, did she or didn't she?" Anna shook her head. Uncle Rolf smiled again and said, "Well, don't frighten me like that. I'll see to it that Aunt Emilia doesn't take either one of you. If I thought she was going to take my Anna away even for a day, I'd shoot her as dead as this partridge." He pulled a snow bird from his pocket and held it out for us to feel, and he said, "Scrawny as Aunt Emilia, eh?" And he laughed and sat down on the clothes chest and yelled, "Frida, Frida, come here and help me!" the way he does every time he comes in. Frida came running from her kitchen in the basement and said, "What is it now again?" though she knows it is always his boots that want pulling off. So then we went away, and Anna said, "That snow bird did look like Aunt Emilia, didn't it?" and we laughed. And because Uncle Rolf had promised to help us, we weren't worried any more. But later in the evening we decided something important in the library. I love the library best of all rooms in Berg, not only because of the books, but because of the big maps on the wall and the huge black bearskins all over the floor, and the smell, and the sound of the mice running behind the shelves squeaking. I am only allowed here because I am a writer and a painter and need that big table for my work. But I don't paint or write most of the time, I play my game. I look and look at the maps and then I go and lie on a bear and play I am in one of those marvelous places I have found written on the map. I make lists of wonderful countries and cities, and the most wonderful, those that I am surely going to travel to, I mark with three stars. Anna doesn't play like that or pretend like that at all. Although she's a year older than me, she usually sits with her dolls on the staircase and is happy, or else she stands about in the garden and is happy there. That evening I was lying on my best bear, the one that has no glass eyes but only two holes for eyes, which makes him look sort of kind and shy. I wasn't doing anything special when I heard Anna walking down the hall, opening and shutting the doors. It's funny how Anna does things. She doesn't run about and call, the way I do when I'm looking for someone. She walks into every room, looks, and walks out again, then looks into the next room, and so on, till she finds me. She walks slowly too, so that sometimes it takes her a very long time to look through both the upstairs and the downstairs rooms for me. When she sat down on my bear I could smell that she had been in the kitchen, for she had a warm sausage-smell. She looked sad and she said, "I have been thinking, have you?" I said, "No, I don't think so."

She said, "Jezza, if Uncle Rolf hadn't spoken to Aunt Emilia for us they would have made you go off to town where everything is crazy. Frida says that everyone runs about and shrieks and quarrels, and talks and talks all the time, and one must wear a hat and one is almost run over every day. We'd have been separated too! And I've been thinking Uncle Rolf won't always be here. It's three years now since his wife, our Aunt Elsa died, and soon Uncle Rolf will have to go back to look after his family's place and stay with his awful brother who is dropsical, and his brother's wife who gives dinner parties. So that's what I've been thinking, that we won't always have Uncle Rolf to speak for us, and they'll take us from each other one day. If Papa and Mama hadn't died in that accident it would be different, but as it is they certainly are going to separate us one day, and then we won't know anything about each other any more. That's why I think we ought to write about what we do each day, and about what we hear and eat and think, so that when we're old ladies we can sit under a tree and read aloud what we've written. Then it won't matter if we have been apart sometimes, because in our books it will say which cow I milked on such and such a day and what sort of lovely food you had for dinner." That was awfully long for Anna to keep talking, for usually she says only a few words. As soon as she stopped I asked her, "When should we begin? I want to write about the reindeer stew we had for lunch." Anna answered,

"Why, right away. I'm going to write on the stair-case." "Good-bye," I said. "But Anna, I am never going to *really* leave you." But then I thought of that lovely name, Quito, riding astride the equator in boilingly hot South America, and I thought of Tre-bizond, far off to the right, and of Lhasa, even farther to the right, and I thought of how I'd love to travel and stare and stare at all three of them. I told Anna, because I always tell her everything. "But anyway," I said, "I have no money for the railroad fares, and we are so far north on the map that railroad fares are terribly expensive, and of course no one in Berg will ever have a krona to spare. I am really more scared about you leaving me, for you have a terribly beau-tiful face and Aunt Emilia says that men run after a beautiful face like mad dogs." Anna said, "Yes, if I keep on getting more beautiful all the time, I'll have to do something to stop it, so they won't make me marry and go away from you. What do you think I could do so as not to be too beautiful?" "You could cut off your curls," I said. "Yes," Anna said, "I could do that." So we got the library scissors, which are dull from cutting string, and we cut all of Anna's curls right off.

4

Anna's Story

I couldn't write on the staircase today because Aunt
Petronella kept walking up and down. Aunt Petronella has bows all the way down her blouse, and lace
cuffs, and a big flowered sash. She wears a ruffle
around her neck. Grandmother says, "Ella is that
kind of a person." That's what Grandmother says,
so I suppose it is all right for her to be like that, only
I wish she wouldn't put bows on the lamp shades
too. Last week when she moved out to Berg from
town to help us prepare for Christmas, she put heaps
of yellow bows around the dining room lamp, so
now it gives hardly any light at all and my staircase
stays dark even with the door into the dining room
open. Too bad she shouldn't have thought of that,
because now the dolls that live on the lower steps sit
around in such darkness they simply can't see a thing.
Of course they can't see anyway, but it's sort of hurt-

ing for them to let on one knows it, as Aunt Petronella
does. Aunt Petronella says I'm too old to play with
dolls, now that we're learning Latin and geometry,
but I can't have children yet so the dolls will have
to do. Anyway, it's Uncle Rolf who makes me have
them. Every time he sends for cigarettes or books
or magazines for himself, he sends for a child for
me. Of course I don't care to explain all that to
Aunt Petronella. It's difficult to talk for those who
don't think it's easy, and besides, no one expects me
to talk, so if I ever do, they all stop to listen, and
that makes it even worse. Grandmother, who always
knows what everyone feels, knew that I went around
feeling angry about Aunt Petronella's bows, and
she said to me, "Anger eats away the flesh of the
soul." She said that to me and then she walked
away, but I kept on standing there looking inside me
and I saw a heap of angry ants eating away my soul.
My soul looked just as thin as a gnawed-off ham-
bone. So then I decided I must never get angry
again, but must do something to fatten up my soul
instead. From then on I have pretended there is very
pale moonlight on my staircase and now the ants
have all stopped gnawing at me. Still it really was
awfully dark, much too dark to sit and write my
book. I went to the library instead, and there was
Jezza painting pictures. She keeps painting faces and
more faces, mostly the faces of people, though I
think animals' faces are better and easier to look into.
She had painted hundreds of these faces on a piece

of paper, and every one of them was looking furious and surprised. "What is it called?" I asked. "People who have lost their train, by Jezza Stark," she answered. I asked, "Why are they so furious? Won't there be another train?" She said, "Of course, in a minute, but when I paint grown-up faces, I always make them furious. That shows right away they are grown-up." I said, "Why don't you stop painting and begin writing our book now, all about what I have said today and the funny songs you made up this morning?" She said, "I don't know how to begin. If I write just what's happened and you write just what's happened, our two books are going to sound the same, because we talk the same, so I suppose that what we write will sound the same too." I said, "It might sound the same, but it isn't going to be the same. Sometimes you're cleaning away dung under Apollo in the stables and talking to Karlson, while I'm in the kitchen thinking, or peeling mushrooms. So you'll write about the dung and I'll write about what I thought in the kitchen, and it won't be the same at all. Do you understand?" "Oh yes," she answered, "now I understand. Get out quick, will you? It's coming. I understand exactly how to write now. Where's my pencil? Oh, I can write wonderfully now." I walked off to the drawing room to see if I could write in there, but the aunts had put fashion books and patterns on every table, and besides, they were running around and whispering and talking to each other, the way they always do. How I'd hate to be their mouths that have to go up and down and open and shut from morning till night, except when their owners are in bed and can't talk any more! Even then I suppose they keep talking, although the sun is put out at night in order to make people shut up. Perhaps that's why our uncles always look gray and sick in the morning and like to go off and sit in a corner by themselves. Well, I went to the sitting room then, and there at the piano was Aunt Helga, practicing her Schubert. When she turned around to see who it was, her pince-nez began slipping off, but that lump at the end of her nose stopped it. It isn't a pretty lump, but it's a great help. Without it her pince-nez would fall off a hundred times a day, because she only thinks of music and forgets all about the pince-nez. She shouted at me, "Oh, get away, get away! Now I have to begin all over again. Do shut the door!" So I went away, and after that there was only the Little Room left to go to, but I heard someone laughing in there and a syphon squirting. It must have been Uncle Rolf having his nightcap with Doctor Borger. I thought of going to Uncle Rolf's office, but some of Uncle Rolf's tramps were sure to be sleeping in there, so there wasn't any point trying. Berg is thick with people. It's crowded now, and it will be much worse in a few weeks when our other aunts and uncles come, and all our cousins, to spend the Christmas holidays. It will be really crazy then. I stood in the hall and didn't know where to go, but just then I saw little Grandmother carrying a flowerpot with one white flower, walking toward her room. I called out, "Grandmother!" and she said, "You want to come to my room, don't you? All right, come along." I walked behind her and I thought of something queer. The door between Grandmother's room and the hall is just an ordinary door, but as soon as it is closed one can't hear a single sound from the whole noisy house! It is quiet, quiet in Grandmother's room, just as it is under a tree. I sat down close to the fire so that I could write by its light, for I know how Grandmother hates lighting the lamps at night. Grandmother does all her reading in the daytime, and at night she sits by her window and looks at the snow outside. She says she has a great love for the snow and that each year she finds out more about it. I said to her once, "Tell me what you see when you sit there looking out." She answered, "Don't you know there are two kinds of people, those who look and those who ask those who look what they are looking at? Don't be one of them! They wouldn't ask if they weren't blind, and it is a crime to be blind like that." I remember everything Grandmother says. I suppose it is easy because she hardly ever says anything, and she never asks questions like other people. For instance, she didn't ask me what I was writing, but when it came time for me to go to bed and I went to curtsy to Grandmother and kiss her thin, thin hand to say good-night, she told me, "Come in here whenever you want to write. Before you start writing, though, stand by the window a little while, looking out. Then there'll be many things that you will not want to write."

5
Jezza's Story

Auntie Ninna keeps coughing in her room. You'd think if she had such a bad cold that she has to cough on hot summer days, to say nothing of all winter, she would be pale and ugly, as one always is when one has a cold, but she isn't pale at all. She is very pink and I love her, for she is terribly gay and just crazy to dance. She is really not like an aunt at all, because she's so young. She is fifteen years younger than our other aunts, and besides, she's not married and full of worries like them. Of course they are gay too, sometimes, but usually they are angry or sad or worried, like all grown-up people. After I'd had my evening bath, the day after Anna and I decided to begin to write, I was going past Aunt Ninna's room, and I stopped to try the handle. The door wasn't locked that day, although usually it is. All our other aunts are always getting furious because of Auntie

Ninna's locking her door. They say that she is secretive. Auntie Ninna screamed at me, "Don't come in!" But then she saw who it was and said, "Oh, it's only Jezza." She was naked, and she was standing in front of her mirror trying on a big hat with feathers and a whole black bird on it, and she looked so sweet. I said to her, "You have lovely breasts, not hanging-down ones, like my other aunts. I hope Anna's and mine will be big and sit up like that when we get them." She asked, "Do you like my hat? I'm going to town with Emilia tomorrow to do my Christmas shopping after all." "Does she know?" I said. "Not yet. I only decided a minute ago," Auntie Ninna answered, and she told me, "Emilia hates having me because I don't get up in the morning, and in her house they want one to get up at dawn. If one's not out of bed by ten, the maid goes crazy and keeps knocking at one's door and saying, 'Oh, I thought you had gone out!'" "Why are you going then?" I asked. "Why, oh why, oh why!" she sang, and she began to dance, and she was so sweet and funny, dancing with no clothes on, only the big feather hat. I sat and looked at all her creams and her bottle of perfume called "Amour-Amour" with a picture on it of a lady with pearls looking terribly hard at a gentleman with a top hat. There was a letter lying on the table from Cousin Staffan with a violet glued to the sheet. I said, "Did Staffan send that to his mother? Aunt Emilia will be glad to get it, won't she?" But as soon as I'd said that, Auntie Ninna came running and grabbed away the letter and she was

furious. She shouted, "Staffan! What do you mean?
I don't know what you mean." I said, "It is Staffan's
handwriting. I was only wondering why he stuck a
violet on it." She said, "It certainly is not Staffan's
handwriting! It isn't, it isn't! Don't you dare go
around now and say it was. Get out!" she shouted at
me. "I didn't ask you to come in here to fuss me.
Can't I try on my hat in peace?" She was terribly
red and her eyes were dark, and then she began to
cough so that her poor sweet breasts hopped up and
down, and she took a towel and spat in it. I wanted
to stay and help her, but she threw her soap at me, so
I ran out. Anna would have hated her for doing that,
but I don't mind. I know just exactly how it feels to
want to throw something hard at someone. "Where
have you been so long?" Anna said when I came back
to our room. She was brushing the short fuzz that
was left on her head after we cut off all the curls.
We thought it was going to make her look ugly, but
it's difficult with Anna—she only gets more and more
beautiful. I wonder why she is so terribly beautiful.
Perhaps it is her eyes, which everyone keeps talking
about, or perhaps it is her soft mouth or her forehead
or her long, long lashes. Anyway, she is so beautiful
that people even speak to her in a different voice
than they use ordinarily. I helped brush her hair
and told her I'd been with Auntie Ninna and helped
her try on her new hat, and there'd been a letter on
the table from Staffan with a violet glued on it.
"What for?"said Anna, and I told her I didn't know
what for.

6

Anna's Story

It's lucky that Uncle Rolf's mare has hoofs instead of feet with soft skin and soft toes. If she'd had feet, she'd have got them frozen off long ago. At ten o'clock every morning Karlson leaves her near the front steps for Uncle Rolf to mount, because ten o'clock is the hour Uncle Rolf plans to leave on his daily inspection tour of Grandmother's fields and of her forests where they are chopping down the trees. The old bailiff is dead and Grandfather is dead too, so there's only Uncle Rolf to look around and see that everything is going right. But the mare waits and waits every morning by those steps and Uncle Rolf doesn't come. He gets waylaid, he says. Everybody wants to speak to him or ask him about some silly nonsense or just joke and have a chat, and Frida keeps talking to him about what she's going to give him to eat that day. It isn't till we've all finished our

breakfasts that he sits down to have his in peace, and
then every morning the maid Karna, while clearing
up the table, says to him, "The mare's been waiting
for two hours now." Then Frida gets furious and
shouts at Karna to shut up—nobody had asked her
to put her nose where it didn't belong. Frida is terribly worried that Uncle Rolf might go out riding
one day before he has finished all of his six eggs. She
says he needs to get up his strength after his twelve
hours' sleep and that it's very tiring to sleep as much
as Uncle Rolf, though she says it's wonderful that
he can do it. She brings up the eggs two at a time so
as to have them piping hot, and hot butter with
them, still hopping about in a dish just as he likes it.
He has six cups of coffee too, and while he is
drinking them, Frida pulls on his riding boots and
grumbles, "The office is full of those tramps again this
morning." She doesn't say that every day, because
the tramps don't come every day, but she says it
pretty often. Sometimes Uncle Rolf gets angry and
says he hasn't time to see them, the mare's been waiting half the morning and he wants some time to himself to read his books and magazines. He complains
a lot, but in the end he always does see them, after
all. He sits down and talks and laughs with them
for hours. And the mare just tosses her lovely head
and waits. This morning after Uncle Rolf had been
in the office a while, Frida sent me in to ask if he
wanted his snow hare done in wine sauce or in lemon
sauce today. Three of the tramps were there, one

whom I don't know very well, and Jonson, whom they call the Scarecrow because all his clothes are stolen off the scarecrows in the fields, and Homer, the Poet. Uncle Rolf's schnapps bottle was on the table and they were just clinking glasses when I came in. When they'd finished drinking, Jonson and the other tramp got up and Uncle Rolf said good-bye to them. Uncle Rolf is wonderfully clever in shaking hands with them. He has a coin in his hand, a krona, and before they know it, it's in their hand, so quick one can't see how it gets there. They always pretend they haven't noticed it, because they know how furious Uncle Rolf gets if they try to thank him. The two tramps said good-bye to me and lifted their caps and grinned. "Good-bye, Fröken Anna," they said. I could see how they hated to leave that lovely hot office and tramp away into the terrible blustering snowstorm. I love the office too— it's such a nice room. It's nice because there's nothing in it, just the hard leather sofa that the tramps sleep on, and the writing desk, and the frightfully hot stove. There's nothing one can break, not even an inkstand, because Uncle Rolf can't bear writing letters. He says only unhappy men write letters and there's no point in keeping accounts, seeing that there's never anything to put on the credit side at Berg. Still, I think there should be an inkstand in an office. The tramps love it in there, with the "Salamander" stove that burns night and day to get the room as hot as Uncle Rolf likes to have it. The front of the stove is always red and I'm sure it's going to melt away soon. When the tramps come to see Uncle Rolf to get their krona and a glass of schnapps, they sit down and thaw out a bit first, and then they take off some rag they've wound about their necks and then another rag under that one, and their old sweaters and the newspapers they pin under their clothes when it's as cold as it is now. Sometimes one of them will sleep the whole day through on the leather sofa, so as to get a real warm sleep. The aunts say it's terrible they should be in there, because it's right next to the sitting room with only a door in between. Uncle Rolf takes no notice of the aunts when they talk like that. Once I heard him say, "Only a woman judges a man by the number of his lice." The only tramp who never takes anything off at all is the one we call Herr Homer, the Poet. Frida says it is because he has nothing on underneath his coat except his trousers and that's why he keeps the coat buttoned right up to his neck and sits almost *on* the stove, so that the sweat simply runs down his face. When the other two had left, he looked at me and said to Uncle Rolf, "I'm off. I'm fleeing away. Lonely roads and icy fields I can bear, they are my lot, but ravaged beauty throws despair into my poet's heart. Whose hand was it that sheared off Fröken Anna's locks?" Uncle Rolf said, "Yes, whose but her sister's, that hell-cat, that limb of Satan! What do you think, Poet? Is her hair ever going to grow out again?" The Poet didn't answer.

He closed his eyes and threw back his head, so I knew some poetry was coming, and I was pleased. He's such a wonderful poet! Jezza and I both loved the verses he wrote for Uncle Rolf's last name day, although the aunts laughed themselves sick at them. Grandmother said that the line about Uncle Rolf which went, "He's a king amongst men for he makes all men kings" was the loveliest thing anyone could have said about anyone. Well, after he had sat there a little while with his eyes shut tight, he opened them and looked at me and said, "North and South have I tramped, and our land is a long land indeed, but did I ever behold a maiden as white and tender and straight at Fröken Anna in Berg? She is a young birch, her hair is the flowing foliage." Then he stopped. Uncle Rolf asked, "And you think that the foliage will one day grow out as long and golden as it was before?" "No, I shouldn't think so," said the Poet, "but there are things that might help. I've heard that it's good to put wet clay on the head and let it dry and stay there for a year. She ought to try that." Uncle Rolf said, "Nonsense! Alcohol's the thing. There's alcohol in all hair tonics, so pure fine alcohol like schnapps ought to make it grow like wildfire." He took up the bottle from the table and pulled out the cork, but the Poet jumped up from his chair and grabbed the bottle away. "No, no, Herr Heller," he said. "Don't play with the gifts of God. I am a man of peace, but I see red when alcohol is treated lightly." Uncle Rolf laughed and made him pour out a glass. The Poet drank it with his hand on his heart, the way he always does, and then he said, "Morpheus has come to visit me. Would it be amiss, Herr Heller, if I leant my weary wanderer's head on your sofa?" "Go ahead, dear fellow," said Uncle Rolf. "Sleep the whole day, if you like, and we'll have a game of whist this evening." Uncle Rolf and I left him in there, but I was sad because he'd said I was so beautiful. I said to Uncle Rolf, "Is it true that I am so terribly beautiful, more beautiful than anyone?" He nodded. I told him, "That's just why Jezza cut off all my hair, so that they won't run after me like mad dogs and make me marry and leave Berg." Uncle Rolf said, "Ah-ha, so that's why she did it! Now I take back every word I said about Jezza. She is a wonderful girl, and I am going to help her fight to keep my treasure in Berg." "Your what?" I asked. And he said, "My own treasure."

7
Jezza's Story

Tomorrow will be the second of December. We never would have known it, because in Berg nobody ever knows the date, but this afternoon when we went into the kitchen to get our ski boots out of the oven, Frida was polishing the big bear gun. Anna grabbed hold of my arm, because the big bear gun is terrible to look at, especially when one knows that it has killed all the bearskins in the library and that huge black one in the hall. Of course, what's even worse is to know that it has sent a bullet into Grandfather's eye and let all of his brains come pouring out. Every year on the first of December Frida polishes the gun, for next day is the second, and that's the anniversary of his death. It was almost dark when we went into the kitchen, but Frida hadn't lit the lamp. She says it's sinful and newfangled to want things always lit up, so she was sitting polishing by the firelight. I

said, "Frida, tell us about the brains on Grandfather's coat and about the 'Last Vikings.'" "Get out
of here, or I'll be aiming this gun at you," said Frida.
"I've got my hands full without your coming here
to pester me, and there's the deer that your Uncle
Rolf shot to be gutted and hung before evening.
Well, what was it that you wanted me to tell you?"
I knew that she remembered perfectly, she only
wanted to be asked again. "Tell us the story about
Grandfather," I said. "It's no story, it's the truth,"
said Frida. "Your grandfather was a great and stout-
hearted man. He was the last real man in the whole
country, and I who am telling you know men from
broken-down hack horses like your city uncles. Well,
aren't you children going to sit down if you want to
hear?" Oh, but I was pleased! We sat down on a
flour sack, and Frida said, "It wasn't as if we hadn't
expected it. Your grandmother always knew it was
going to happen." "How did she know that, Frida?
How could she know that Grandfather was going to
shoot himself?" I asked. "I've told you a hundred
times," Frida said. "Naturally she knew that her
own husband belonged to the Last Vikings, of which
there was only a handful still alive, and, like all of
them, he'd sworn to 'live like a man and die like a
man.' When one of these Last Vikings felt old age
stealing up behind him, when he was getting hard of
hearing or had begun to drop his teeth, he coaxed
up his courage and went to get his gun, not wanting
to die in a soft bed like a woman. No, that wouldn't

have been a proper viking's death, and these men had the spirit of vikings and they wanted to die as such. Well, the Sunday morning I was busy raking the ashes out of the hall stove. It was five o'clock and black as black. Suddenly, I heard a sound in the next room, and when I went in, there was your grandfather taking the bear gun off the wall. I thought it was funny he should go bear shooting on a Sunday, but before I could say anything, he was right beside me, had taken hold of my hand and pressed it hard. I couldn't see him, it was so dark, but his hand was warm and his clasp stronger than any I'd ever felt before. In a second he was gone, and then all at once it came to me what he meant to do. I remembered that lately he'd begun to hold his book closer and closer to his eyes to read, and I also remembered the queer way he'd taken to looking at your lovely grandmother, just as if he couldn't feast his eyes on her enough. I thought, 'He's gone to the forest!' and I was about to run after him when I stopped myself. I thought if he hadn't known me to be a woman who can hold her tongue, then he'd have gone off without farewell. I felt proud then and I went about my work, saying nothing." Frida didn't say anything now either, but just sat for a moment polishing the gun barrel. She rubbed and rubbed with her chamois, and the barrel shone in the firelight and looked terribly dangerous. After a moment I thought she'd forgotten all about us, so I said, "You'd got to where you felt proud and went about your work.

What happened afterwards, Frida?" She said, "Karlson came running. Karlson was young then, and he rushed into the kitchen, looking wild. 'Master's lying in the forest!' he shouted. 'He's lying by the big pine tree with a bullet in his head.' I didn't let out a word, and I didn't rush off in every direction, like most womenfolk would have done. I got a towel and a clean sheet and walked deep into the forest and up to the giant pine tree. The cold was fierce that winter. It was forty degrees below zero and the wolves had come down, barking, from the mountains. Millions of stars were out and they twinkled in the cold. There by the big pine tree lay your grandfather, stretched out like a fallen tree himself."
"With brains on his coat?" I asked Frida, but she got angry and said, "You keep fussing me about those brains on his coat. Yes, why shouldn't they have been on his coat, seeing that he'd blown them right out of his skull? He'd stuck the butt of his gun in the snow so that he could put his head against the barrel and push the trigger with his boot, for he wanted to die by the gun that had been such a true friend to him. I washed him with snow and then we carried him home to your grandmother." "Poor Grandmother!" Anna said, and Frida said, "Poor? You mean lucky. Lucky to be the chosen wife of a man as brave as a viking, lucky to have six children by him. I don't call that being poor! Ask your grandmother why she keeps to herself and is always silent. After living with a giant, ordinary people seem

small. She doesn't want to waste words on chattering magpies like your aunts. "Aren't you going to tell us about Pastor Petrus now?" I asked. "And how he called Grandfather a suicide and wouldn't let him lie in hallowed ground?" But Frida said, "I haven't got time, with the venison waiting to be cleaned. And if I once began to think of that miserable creature, that old woman in pants, Pastor Petrus, I'd get into such a state I'd slash the meat until it wasn't fit to eat. No more fit to eat than that sniveling pastor is fit to live!" Anna asked, "Are all pastors sniveling and not fit to live?" Frida answered, "Certainly not, but Pastor Petrus is. Your own grandfather used to say so, and if anyone had the right to judge, I suppose it was a Last Viking, who understood how to live and who understood how to die too, when the time came."

8

Anna's Story

All of Berg smells of food now, of sausages and new-made cakes and beer, and the smells have to stay indoors, because the house is all sealed up. The big Christmas cold has come, and everything out of doors is stiff. The lake is frozen right through and everything inside of it is dead. In every room a stove is burning crazily and Karna runs around cramming their mouths full of logs all day, and even at night she has to get up to do it. The double windows have been put in and all the cracks stopped with cotton to keep the snowstorms from blowing in. There is no one in any of the upstairs rooms because all are in the kitchen preparing the Christmas food, and it's just crazy down there now with everyone laughing and running about. I like it much better when Frida and I make food alone. Frida says that I'll become a great cook one day and that I have a special hand with food. I suppose that's because I love food so much, not only to eat it, but to handle it, too. I love big pink carrots with dew in their hair and earth on their feet and strong-smelling parsley, and red meat and bowls of thick cream, and round gay mushrooms. They're all alive, not dead, like the other things we see and handle—I mean pencils and books and sewing needles. I like to bathe the earth off the carrots' feet and to put them to boil in salt bubbling water, and I love to squeeze the fine parsley leaves and sniff them, and peel the round white mushrooms whose skin always sticks to my fingers. While I am chopping or cutting up or peeling the food I get to know all about it, and I think of how I want each thing to taste, and how I'd like to prepare it. For instance, peas are little and kind, and want a kind sauce to lie in, while cabbage is strong and angry and wants heaps of spices, and fish should taste of the wild sea and be served on the leaves of that bush that smells so crazily, and meat is live and red and should taste live and red. Frida has taught me everything she knows, but when I think differently from her, she tells me that maybe I am right and she is wrong. Lovely Frida! We never talk, for each of us stays working in her own corner in our huge kitchen, but we love each other the whole time. It is the best thing in the world to work with someone and not to talk, because when there are no awful talking-voices, then I can hear all the other voices in the room. The voice of the oil in the lamp makes a nice spitting sound, and the logs in the fireplace lie beside each other and whisper. The chopper has an even, little voice as it goes up and down on the table. Of course it isn't quiet and peaceful in the kitchen just now, with ten people or more making Christmas dishes and all of them so gay! This afternoon when the room was like a steam bath because of the steam from the big hams boiling on the range, Uncle Rolf came in with a second hat of snow on top of his high pointed bearskin cap. "At this moment they are wringing the necks of twenty geese," he told us. "Can you hear them quacking? Tomorrow we'll start making goose-liver *pâté*s." Frida screamed as if she were having her neck wrung too. "Twenty! Why, during the thirty years that I've been cook at Berg, I've never used more than ten goose livers in the Christmas *pâté*s. We've never killed more than ten, have we, Fru von Stark?" she asked, turning to Grandmother. Uncle Rolf laughed and said, "Did I say twenty? Well, I made a mistake, Frida. I didn't mean twenty but thirty. At this very moment they're wringing the neck of the thirtieth goose, and what's more, they have orders to go on until I tell them to stop." "Heavens!" shrieked Frida, and she ran up to Grandmother, who was sitting sorting spices at a little table in the corner under the nice yellow lamp. "Please do something, Fru von Stark," she said. "To chop thirty goose livers up fine would simply be the death of me!" "Not to mention the pounds and pounds of bacon lean and bacon fat that's to be chopped up with it," said Uncle Rolf, "and huge jars of chopped-up gherkins." "There are no gherkins going into my *pâté*!" shouted Frida. "If you flay me alive, not a single gherkin is going in." "Not into your *pâté* but into mine, perhaps," said Uncle Rolf, and he tied on an apron and put a dust cloth around his head, and then he grabbed hold of Frida and began to dance with her, singing, "Oh, when the ball is over, Oh, when the lights are out!" They danced and danced, and it was easy to see how Frida adored Uncle Rolf. Then he set her down on top of the big kitchen cupboard. He's so terribly tall that it's nothing for him to reach up there. I put a chair underneath so that Frida could limb down, for she's very old, even older than Grandmother, and she can't jump. Frida said, "We're better off when we're alone, aren't we, my quiet mouse?" But her eyes were all dancy and gay, and she went away and came back with a whole armful of salt gherkins from the larder.

9
Jezza's Story

Baldur died today. It's nicer to say died, but he didn't really die, he was shot. The vet looked at his teeth and saw how old he was, so he told Karlson, the coachman, to shoot him, and he did. "You might at least have waited till after Christmas when you knew how terribly I loved him," I said to Karlson, but Sven, who was wheeling out dung from the pigsty, said, "That would have been too late. The butcher wants to make Christmas sausage out of him, good tough old horse sausage." I couldn't help laughing, but Anna didn't laugh. She said to Karlson, "That isn't a bit true, is it?" Karlson answered, "Yes, Sven is right. The horse wouldn't have lasted out another month, and even Sven knows that." Well, if even Sven knows it, then I suppose it must be true, because Sven is a half-wit and looks just like a little boy, though he's over forty. He's so small he can run under the horses' bellies when he cleans their stalls, and can almost stand upright under the two biggest horses, Hector and Ajax. All Sven can do is wheel out dung and he's been doing that ever since he was ten years old. For thirty years Sven had been wheeling out dung, and I'm sure if he wasn't simple in the head he'd have learned to do something else by now. Still, he wasn't simple enough not to know about Baldur and the sausages, and he winked at me when he said it. I winked back. I like Sven, and he likes me too, for I always ask him what time it is and that gives him a chance to take out the silver watch his father gave him when he heard him fiddle his three tunes. People in Berg never could guess how Sven managed to learn those tunes, because they didn't know that Sven was the son of the great fiddler Sven, in Hamar. When our Sven was young, before he became so simple, he lived with his father, and that is when he learned to play the fiddle, or rather when he learned to play his three tunes on the fiddle. Since then old Sven moved to Hamar and he never came to Berg because he was so ashamed of his son. Besides, he had swollen legs and couldn't have limped all the way down the hill. Sven, our Sven, was so simple that he had forgotten all about his father, but last August Sven in Hamar sent word to Berg that there was something called gangrene in his legs and he couldn't last out the winter, so he wanted to have a look at his son. Frida said she would take him over. She has a niece in Hamar, in fact she has a niece in almost every village, and she knew that Sven was much too simple to find his way there alone. How sad she must have been to show the big fiddler-Sven such an idiot as our dung-Sven, looking just like a little boy and smelling terribly of the stable and the pigsty, even though Frida had lent him a brush to scrub off the very worst! They started off from Berg before it was light, as Frida can't hurry because of her breath, and when they had been walking about an hour he ran away from her. Poor Frida hobbled after him, but he had only run back to Berg to fetch his fiddle, so they started off again, in the daylight this time. Frida says it was lucky he did run home, for when they finally arrived and fiddler-Sven and dung-Sven had said how-do-you-do, they had nothing more to talk about, seeing that they hadn't seen each other for thirty years. Our Sven just stood staring at his feet, and his father, who couldn't stand, sat in a chair staring at his feet too. Then suddenly dung-Sven realized he was holding his fiddle in his hand, and he began to play, for, Frida says, he must have known that his fiddle is his voice. Frida says he played so wonderfully. He played about the summertime, she says, about the long summer days in Berg, and she could actually *see* the strawberries and their warm curly leaves, and the round clouds walking over the sky. He played and played. I suppose he had heaps to tell his father. Perhaps he wanted to say how achingly sad he was always to have to wheel dung, or to tell his father how it felt when everybody laughed at him. I can just imagine all the sad things he had to say, only he had to say them all by playing because he can't put sentences together but mixes them all up and begins to splutter and spit. Frida says that as he played she could see old Sven getting happy all over, and he sat and listened to every note as it came out of dung-Sven's fiddle, so clear and round and fine. When he finished, his father got out his own wonderful fiddle and he began to play the tunes that he had once made famous and that Frida had listened to when she was a young girl. She said, though she'd heard him many times at the grandest weddings and midsummer parties, she'd never heard him play to other people so grandly as he did that day to his son. He must have tried his very hardest because he knew that now he was playing to someone who understood music better than anyone on earth. When he stopped at last, dung-Sven played his three tunes again, and then his father played some more, and then dung-Sven played, and it was so beautiful that Frida thought she must be dead and was sitting in heaven. She decided she would have a cry, and she did. She had a good long one. Frida says that's a good thing to do every fifth year, not oftener because it makes one mushy, but every fifth year one has got together enough really to cry about. Frida sat and cried away her last five years, and she felt so happy. They played and played to each other all day long. When one stopped, then the other started. The stars came out and they were still playing. Frida hated to break in on them, but at last she told Sven that they would have to be going. Sven got up, for he always does just what he's told, like a little boy, and he said good-bye to his father, and that was all they had said to each other, though they hadn't met for thirty years, just how-do-you-do and good-bye. His father shook hands with Sven and looked at him a long time, and then he took off his big silver watch and put it in Sven's hand. All the way home that night Sven kept smiling. Frida says every star was out and it was a glittering light night, so she could see Sven's face the whole way, and there wasn't a moment that his face wasn't smiling. She says Sven has never looked really sad since that day, and it's Frida who told us always to ask him the time as soon as we see him. So that's the story of Sven's watch and that's why he likes me for asking him the time, even though he should have known better than to tell me about Baldur's being made into sausage. Because I couldn't help laughing at what he'd said, Anna didn't want to play with me—not that she said anything to me about it, but I felt it. I went to the cow shed and thought of poor Baldur and of our dog, Gorm the Fifth, whom they also had to shoot last summer because he was stiff as a stick from old age. It was pitch-black in the cow shed, it was four o'clock already, and they were milking the cows. I love to sit there when it's dark, with only the lanterns burning at either end of the long low shed, and listen to the cows chewing and smell the warm smell. I know from the sound the milk makes when it runs into the pail exactly which cow Bengta or Fru Boberg or Gudrun is milking. I went to Bengta and said, "May I milk my cow?" "No," she said, "you only worry her." "No, I don't, Bengta," I said. "You do too," she said. "You don't come here regularly, like Fröken Anna does, and the cow's milk gets all upset when you do her one day and I do her the next. You leave milk in her udder too. You don't finish her off properly." I said, "If I do that it's because her back paps are so short I can't take a real pull at them." "Wet them with milk as I've told you to," she said. I asked her, "Let me try now," but she still said no. "You're mean not to want me to have a little fun when I'm so terribly sad about Baldur," I said. She asked me, "What?" and I said, "Don't you know that Karlson shot Baldur behind the tool shed because he was so awfully old, just like Gorm last summer?" But then I remembered that Bengta is even older than Gorm or Baldur and that she can only milk ten cows now, while Fru Boberg and Gudrun take twenty each. Bengta's chin trembles all the time and she hasn't a single hair left on her head. I thought I ought to say something, so I said, "We won't shoot you, Bengta, we'll let you die of old age, darling." She patted my head and looked so kind and said, "Bless you, child." And then a little later she said, "You milk the white cow. She has four good paps."

10

Anna's Story

The letter has come now, so there's no point in hoping it won't come, because it *has* come. We were all sure it would, seeing that it always comes around Christmas time—still, there was no harm in wishing that it wouldn't. This morning when Jezza and I went to the kitchen to get our ski boots out of the oven, Frida threw them at us and shouted, "Must you clutter up my kitchen with your smelly old goatskin boots?" So we knew there was something wrong, because it's she herself who dries them and greases them and shines their buckles and is so wonderful to them. "Now they are after him again," said Frida. "After him? After whom?" Jezza asked, but I had guessed already. "And they have to use cream-colored writing paper with a crest, although they don't belong to the nobility, as your grandmother does," Frida went on without answering. "Why can't they write on white paper like other folk? Oh no, cream-colored paper is much finer, cream-colored paper as thick as wallpaper, and the envelope stuck together so tight it's the devil's own job to open it! Why can't they think of other people once in a while? Not everyone has fifteen minutes to spare to steam open envelopes." "Oh, it was from Uncle Rolf's family, wasn't it?" asked Jezza. Of course Frida opens everybody's letters before they do themselves, so she knows better than anybody just what's happening in the family. She was so angry this morning that she gave the door of the kitchen stove an awful kick and Jezza began to laugh. "That's right, laugh away," said Frida, furious. "There won't be much laughter, though, when they take your handsome young uncle away from us. That's what they're going to do. His older brother who has the dropsy says he'll cut out your Uncle Rolf unless he comes back to look after the estate. Bah! As if Berg wasn't his own home more than any other place could ever be." "How do you know all that?" said Jezza, and Frida said, "How do I know? Don't you think that I can read? And this time he's really going to go. Nothing lucky will happen to stop him, like all the other times. We're going to lose him now for good. I feel it in my bones." Frida's bones feel an awful lot, nearly always the wrong thing, but still I got so achingly sad I had to stop on every step on my way upstairs. I got all heavy, I was so sad. I didn't want my breakfast any more, so I went out of doors, though I didn't have anything special to do there. I stood about a little and I shook a bush and a lot of snow fell off. For lunch Frida had made stuffed cabbage and veal in mushroom sauce and raw eggs with anchovies, all things that Uncle Rolf thinks are splendid, and he ate a lot of everything, for he always has such a beautiful appetite. Frida is so proud of his fine huge appetite she cooks three or four extra dishes for him every day, and he eats them all. Grandmother looks at him when he eats, and smiles and nods to him. The table is always covered with lovely-smelling side dishes and glittering china and silverware and pitchers of cream and jugs of beer, and everyone eats away, talking and laughing a lot. But right at the head of the table sits little Grandmother, not saying a word and only eating one single potato and a salt herring for lunch the whole year around, never anything else. She is so strict with herself, but she doesn't fuss at other people who aren't like her, not a bit. Today Uncle Rolf ate everything sadly and we all knew he was thinking that this was the last time he'd get real, thick Berg mushroom sauce. Everyone sat there looking heavy with the sad thoughts they were thinking. It was my day to read him to sleep for his after-lunch snooze, though of course I never really read, like Jezza does on her days. I can't do that, for it's so awful to say things aloud. Uncle Rolf understands this. In summer I sit and swish away the flies, and in winter I just sit. When I came in today he wasn't in his dressing gown, which I love best of all clothes in the world because it is of thick red velvet and very long and full. He was walking about with his riding breeches and riding boots still on, carrying piles of underwear and socks and putting them down somewhere and then taking them up again and putting them down somewhere else. The room was full of trunks and boxes. I wanted to say something to him about money, because of Frida's telling us that his brother wouldn't give him any more if he stayed with us in Berg. It's too bad I never know what to say. I took my krona piece out of my purse, the krona I'd got for shoveling snow, and I put it on the table. Uncle Rolf stood and looked and looked at it. I don't know what he could have been thinking of. Then he took it in his hand and kissed it and came over to me and put it back in my purse. He buttoned the purse and put it back in my pocket and he said, "I don't want money, my darling. What should I do with money? A happy man doesn't need money." He went and looked out of the window, though there was nothing to see outside but walls of ice covered with snow from the last big snowfall, and anyway the pane was so full of ice flowers he couldn't have seen through it at all. After a moment he said, "It isn't because of money that I'm leaving. I came to Berg once, a man like any other man in the world, poor with money. I have learned something here. I have learned to be a happy man." He left the window and walked over to the fireplace and began poking the logs with his boot. That's why Frida can't get the toes of his boots to shine, though she spits in the shoe polish and uses a chamois cloth she keeps especially for Uncle Rolf's boots. They'll never shine as they should as long as he keeps poking at the logs. "Today," said Uncle Rolf, "my skinflint brother sent me eight pages in tiny handwriting, saying such ugly things that none of you people here in Berg would even know what they meant. I'm ashamed before poor old Frida because she read them." He didn't say any more right away, but stood looking into the fire. Then he said, "There won't be any big blazing Berg fires for me any more. Nobody laughs down in my home, they don't know how to. If Jezza had one of her fits of gaiety, the tapestries and the famous paintings would come tumbling down! It's such an orderly place, and the neighbors drive over for visits, and then at dinner one has to wear a stiff shirt and chat away with ugly ladies covered with powder." I heard steps outside, angry steps, and it was Frida who came stamping in looking just like she had this morning when she kicked the stove for no reason except that her foot had a lot of anger in it. She wouldn't look at Uncle Rolf, but she said to me, "Here's a warm undervest for your uncle. Mind that he doesn't lie down in the sweaty one he used for riding. And here's a pitcher of hot spiced wine. He needs a good long nap to strengthen him for his cruel journey tomorrow and for all the awful things he's going back to." She sniffed terribly and banged the door behind her so that the smoke from the fire blew out into the room, and she hadn't looked once at Uncle Rolf. I said, "Uncle Rolf!" and held the dressing gown and the vest out to him. "Well," he said, "I'm not sure if I ought to take a nap today. Perhaps I'd better pack and start getting into training for that slave's life I'll have to lead. Nobody ever takes a nap down there. They don't need it because they don't drink or eat properly but only sit nibbling at fancy food and keeping up a cultured conversation." Still, he did get into his vest. Every morning, Frida warms Uncle Rolf's underwear and socks, hanging them on thyme twigs in the stove. That's why he always smells so lovely and fresh, like a huge tree in the forest. He wrapped his thick red dressing gown about him and he looked so wonderful, and as young as a boy. Then he got into bed. I settled down at the foot of the bed as I always do, and oh, it's such a huge warm lovely bed, built just like a house, with a real ceiling above! He didn't close his eyes today but just lay and looked and looked at me and drew some figures in the air with his finger, and he said, "Golden butterflies fluttering about her head, eyelashes like feathers, soft lips that stay ever silently shut." "Is that me, Uncle Rolf?" I asked. He said, "No. It's someone I dream about, someone I love."

11

Jezza's Story

Someone ought to murder Aunt Helga. At least that's what my other aunts say, because then she'd stop practicing her awful Schubert. I think that's silly, and I think it's fine of Aunt Helga to keep on loving him so and trying and trying to become a concert pianist. Last summer she knew only three parts of the Concerto, but by now she knows more or less the whole five, and at Christmas when all the fun begins she is going to play it right through for us, from beginning to end. Everyone says they are looking forward to hearing it but that it's too bad her touch is so hard, although she has a wonderful ear. It makes me furious that people who can't do anything at all always peck at someone who can. I asked Frida, "Do you think that Aunt Helga's touch is hard?" "How should *I* know?" said Frida. So that wasn't much help, but I don't think her touch is too hard at all. Aunt Helga gets absolutely crazy if you disturb her when she's playing, so I sometimes hide beneath the piano before she comes in, and she can't see me because of the big rose-colored cloth that hangs down to the floor. The only person who is allowed to listen to her is one of Uncle Rolf's tramps, Torkel, who suffers from the Arctic disease. Aunt Helga says it is a sort of crazy sadness that people who live near the Arctic get because it is pitch-black nine months of the year. By mistake Torkel's old father once skied out onto the frozen Arctic Seas and was never seen again, and Torkel's mother stood staring after him, crying, for nine coal-black months till her eyes went blind. Only she never knew it, as it was always dark around her anyway, so she just kept on staring and weeping, and Torkel couldn't stand it and skied southwards. But by then he had already caught the Arctic disease, and he was picked up somewhere and put in a madhouse. After he got out, he just wandered about and never spoke to anyone, but he often comes to Berg and sits in Uncle Rolf's office with the door open to the sitting room, listening to Aunt Helga playing her Concerto. And all the while he listens, he keeps crocheting, as he learned to do in the lunatic asylum. It's a huge shawl he works on, and he crochets it full of red apples and oranges and birds as blue as the sky in summer, all sorts of things that aren't sad and black, as things are in the terrible Arctic. We all think he is going to give it to Aunt Helga when it's

finished. Often when I sit under the piano I watch
him from under the cloth that hangs far down, and
I see that his terribly sad face gets all limbered up as
Aunt Helga plays. No wonder, for it's heavenly
when she makes the piano boom and shake and really
weep or laugh. Then the lovely music puts its arms
around one and squeezes one hard! But after Aunt
Helga has got her piano really worked up, she
soothes it by stroking the keys with her strong, quiet
fingers, and then she sits looking straight before her,
and Torkel sits staring at his oranges, and I am so
limp and happy I have to kiss myself under the
piano. The other day I was singing the last part of
the Concerto while I shoveled snow to earn those ten
öre that are still missing from my krona. Suddenly
Aunt Helga stuck out her head and shouted, "How
did you learn that music?" I was feeling awfully
gay, the way one gets to feel from singing alone very
loudly, and it didn't seem to matter if she knew. I
shouted back," I hid under the piano!" Aunt Helga's
face is tired and white because she always stays indoors playing, and trying so crazily to become a concert pianist. It looked like a white cheese hanging
out of the window. Her eyes are all screwed up from
reading tiny little music, and if she weren't tall and
sort of elegant like all the other aunts, you'd never
think she was one of Grandmother's daughters. She
pushed her hair away, the way she does, and then
she took off her pince-nez and rubbed her eyes. She
let her hand, which is big and beautiful and sad, stay

over her eyes for a little while, and then she took it away and she began to hum the lovely music that I'd just been singing, and we smiled at one another. Then all at once we began to like each other! It was just like that. So, since then I'm allowed to sit with her when she practices, and she tells me all about Schubert, another bit about him every day, but not at all in the same voice she uses when she talks to my other aunts or to Uncle Viktor, who's her husband and who's wheezy and has such colds in the head he uses up eighteen handkerchiefs a day, which have to be made of the finest linen, coming from Ireland beside England, because his nose is all worn out and raw as beef from being blown and blown all the time. It's a shame she couldn't have married Schubert instead of Uncle Viktor. Perhaps she'd talk with that lovely rich voice all the time then, and be happy and magnificent, the way I think people ought to be. She said to me, "Of course your singing voice is simply atrocious, child, but you're an artist. One can see that from your bumpy forehead. You and I have artist's foreheads." I said, "Are we pleased that I'm an artist, or aren't we pleased?" and she answered, "Child, don't you know that all people are divided into two classes, the artists and the ordinary ones? They are easy to know apart, and I'll tell you how. Every artist has a wing on his back, and the great soaring artists have two. Ordinary people never have wings, and usually they are clubfooted besides. That's why they walk so queerly. Haven't you ever watched the way people walk, heavy, heavy, heavy!" I said, "Yes, I have noticed." But then I thought of Anna and I asked, "What about Anna? She isn't an artist, is she?" "Ah, Anna!" said Aunt Helga, and she smiled sort of secretly, and I saw that Aunt Helga knew all about Anna's being different from anyone on earth. So now Aunt Helga has really become my darling. Best of all I love Auntie Ninna, of course, and now Aunt Helga comes next and then Aunt Petronella, and last of all Aunt Emilia. I just can't bear Aunt Emilia! She is always ordering people about, and that is why everyone calls her "Field Marshal Stark," after Great-great-grandfather Stark, who really was a field marshal. At afternoon coffee today, when we were eating the broken pastry left over from the Christmas pastry making, the snow began to blow around and hit the windows, and Aunt Emilia said, "The wind sounds like a pack of wolves. Rolf had better start early for his boat tomorrow. The snow is five yards high." Fancy talking about that awfully sad thing, just when we were having coffee and sampling the Christmas pastry and trying to be a little gay and to forget! Aunt Helga said, "Oh, you *must* rub it in of course!" and I loved her awfully for saying that. The Field Marshall answered, "You're all scatterbrains. Don't you realize what our brother-in-law Rolf stands to lose? His money and property are at stake, and I ask you, what is a man without money and property?" Nobody answered, but they all looked toward Grandmother to see what she would say. She didn't say anything, only put her arm tight around Anna and looked into the fire. Nobody wanted those cakes any more—that is, no one except me. Aunt Helga said, "Oh, when I think of his poor tramps! His poor poet! What is going to happen to them now?" "They can tramp after him," said Auntie Ninna. "They're luckier than we are. They haven't got a house, and their only luggage is their bugs. They travel light, but poor we will have to sit here and never see the sight of Rolf again." Aunt Helga said, "His poet will miss him most, though they will all miss him. Alms and drink they might get elsewhere, but they'll never find that something that Rolf gives away with every gift he makes. That something that makes one want to walk straight into his arms!" Grandmother looked up quickly and said, "Shall I tell you Rolf's secret? Shall I tell you why he is so loved? It's because courteously, with complete sincerity, he bows before the inner man he sees in every person that he talks to." She looked at Aunt Ninna and at Aunt Helga and said, "Your eyes are shining. That proves I was right." The door opened then, and it was Uncle Rolf himself who came in. I ran to pull out his special chair for him by the fire, but he didn't want it. "If you could only stay over Christmas, Uncle Rolf!" I said. "*Neptune III* makes her last trip tomorrow," he answered. "Everything's freezing up and there won't be another boat till the ice breaks in the spring. As to sitting on a stuffy train for twenty-four hours, staring at a lot of ugly faces, no thank you! On board the steamer, I'll have clean salt air blowing in my face, and I've a feeling for that captain on *Neptune III*. He takes his drinking seriously, he's an estimable fellow. Now I think we'll talk of something else." He carried his cup of coffee to the window. I suppose it was so that we shouldn't see his face. Aunt Emilia said, "Poor Rolf, I know just how you feel! Although all of us live far away, yet each year we still come running home for Christmas. Our hearts would break if we couldn't spend every Christmas and every summer here." Aunt Helga nudged her so that she would stop and not make Uncle Rolf sadder still, but then she said something even worse. It was just typical of the Field Marshall! "I suppose that Staffan will be riding your little mare now," she said. "He's always had his eye on her." Uncle Rolf jumped up, upsetting his coffee cup, and the coffee ran over the carpet, right into the face of a rose. His eyes were black and furious. "He's had his eye on her, has he?" he shouted. "As if that idiot knew the difference between a hack and a thoroughbred! Why, I'd shoot the mare dead rather than have him mount her! Him or anybody else. Shoot her dead as a doornail!" He tore out of the room and a moment later the front door banged so that the whole house shook.

12

Anna's Story

I thought it was still night when the gong began to boom. Then I remembered it was meant to wake us for Uncle Rolf's departure! I couldn't move at all, and if I moved the slightest bit, I was so sad that it hurt. I didn't hear Jezza get out of her bed, but all at once she popped up under my blanket and put her face next to mine. She began to cry, just because I was so sad, but I was much too sad to cry. Then she went to get my undervest and drawers, and she sat on them to warm them, and she pulled on my stockings for me, although I am a year older. I kept thinking, it can't be true that tomorrow when we're having breakfast Uncle Rolf won't come in with his red, red bedroom slippers on! Perhaps if I close my eyes and then open them again, I'll find out that it isn't true. Well, I did that, closed my eyes and then opened them, and it still was true. When we got downstairs, they were all standing by the front door. Grandmother went to fetch the bottle of coconut oil, and we all smeared our faces and especially our ears, because it was twenty degrees below zero and we had a long trip ahead of us. It was still pitch-dark outside, with only a few stars out, and none of us looked at each other or even said good-morning. It was terrible. Jezza kept her arm about my neck the whole time, even while we were drinking our coffee. Uncle Rolf came in. He said, "Where's my old Frida? I've been looking for her everywhere to say good-bye." "Frida's locked herself up in the cellar," said Grandmother. "She keeps weeping and howling. She won't come out until you've gone away because she can't bear to say good-bye. You'd better be leaving now, my boy." Nobody talked in the sleigh and we could scarcely breathe, it was so cold. Jezza and I made a house on the floor beneath the bearskin rugs, but then I remembered that I was never going to see Uncle Rolf again, so I had to make a peephole to look out at him. He had made a sort of house for himself too by pulling down his fur cap and pushing up his fur collar. All I could see of him was one eye, all black and not looking like Uncle Rolf's eye at all. Behind us we heard the bells from the second sleigh with all of Uncle Rolf's luggage, and those bells sounded stupidly gay, tinkling away without understanding how terrible it was that all of Uncle Rolf's darling clothes were leaving Berg, even his red dressing gown, which smells so heavenly of thyme. I wished they would keep quiet but they wouldn't. I put my fingers in my ears. Our own sleigh was just heavy with sadness, and it seemed as if we weren't moving at all but staying in the same horrid place all the time. Uncle Rolf couldn't stand it either. He jumped up all at once and swung himself up into the driver's seat and grabbed the reins from Karlson. "Don't you know how to drive?" he yelled. "You old slowpoke! I'm not going to miss the boat and have this nightmare trip to do over again. It's bad enough just once." He gave the horses all the rein they wanted and stood up and drove like that, whipping them about their legs so that they began to gallop, quick as hares. The sleigh flew along, dancing from one side of the road to the other because it was so icy. Karlson's cap blew off, the wind bit at my ears, and all the aunts began to shriek because they knew we were getting near the big hill leading to the lake. And then, when we were right at the top, the horses bolted to one side. They left the road and dashed across a field and then into another field, and across that one too. I knew then they were running away with us, and lumps of snow from their hoofs flew into our faces. There was a crunch and a huge bang, and I felt myself flying out of the sleigh. Of course I didn't know that we had run into a covered-over stone pile, but now I know that's what happened. When I opened my eyes, everybody was crawling about in the snow and looking for everybody else. Uncle Rolf came running up to me. He felt my legs to see if they weren't broken off, and then he felt me all over and he began to kiss me. Nobody was hurt and in a few miuntes they all began to laugh, and of course Uncle Rolf laughed louder than anyone, he always does. "Oh, what's happened to my pince-nez?" said Aunt Helga, sitting in the snow with her hat on one ear. "I'm blind as a bat without them. Won't somebody find my pince-nez for me?" So that made us all laugh even more, and Uncle Rolf found them and stuck them back on Aunt Helga's nose, but the glasses had broken off and there was just the gold part left. "What about the boat?" said Aunt Emilia. She would say that! "What boat?" shouted Uncle Rolf. "I've missed *Neptune III* and now there isn't another boat until the spring. What a fool I was to think of leaving Berg! Why should I leave the place where my heart has learned to laugh?" The sleigh was broken and both horses had run away, so we started trudging homeward through the snow. The stars winked at us and we all walked arm in arm. It got light and we were all terribly happy.

13
Jezza's Story

Yesterday my feet were crazy with that sort of hoppy feeling. Anna was stuffing Christmas sausages with the others. She likes working. Some do, some don't. I don't. I waited around outside the kitchen door for Auntie Ninna to come out, but I took care no one should see me, otherwise they'd have put me to stuffing sausages or peeling almonds. When Auntie Ninna came out, I grabbed hold of her and pulled her down the passage. I asked her, "Couldn't we do something? I feel so hoppy and funny today." "I, too," she said. "I feel terribly gay, and I refuse to stuff another sausage. What can we do, though?" Just then someone began calling, "Ninna! Ninna!" and Auntie Ninna grabbed hold of my hand and we hid behind the cellar door until they stopped calling her. She said, "How I love to run away, don't you? Everyone's always trying to catch me to make me

settle down or to make me do this or make me do
that, but they haven't got me yet, have they?" I
said, "If I don't have some fun, I'll burst. Do you
know how I feel? My legs have been crazy all day."
"Mine have too," said Auntie Ninna, "but then
they're always like that. Listen, do you want me to
teach you the fox trot? We can run over to the
doctor's and play his gramophone and I'll teach you
the fox trot." We got our overcoats, but we didn't
have time to find our overshoes, for there was someone coming. The snow was as high as tall houses,
and I thought of Auntie Ninna's cough and said,
"You shouldn't go out without your overshoes," but
she answered, "What does it matter? The snow feels
lovely after that hot kitchen. Talking of shoes," she
said, "did I ever tell you about my magic slippers?
They were made of silver cloth and they had high,
high heels and bows like little butterflies, and they
were, oh, so thin! I got them for my first big ball
and whenever I had them on I used to have such
tremendous fun. They were light as air and of course
I wore them to a shred. Next year I got another
pair, this time of good solid kid, because my sisters
kept telling me they'd last better. Well, you know
how I hate things that last. And can you believe it,
that year I had no fun at all? At dances I didn't
have half of my old success." "Why didn't you use
the old ones again?" I asked. "That's just what I
did do," said Aunt Ninna, and she laughed as if she
had a lot of tinkling bells inside her. "I had them

recovered with silver cloth and I used to fly away on them and dance all night. All my old power was back again! There was magic in those shoes. Even standing in the cupboard, so light, so elegant, they seemed to be saying, 'We're off for some fun!' and I understood them, for that's what I always feel like saying, too. I always want to be off for some new fun, Jezza!" The doctor's dog came running out to bark at us. He's the father of our dog, Gorm the Sixth, we think, but bitches have such a lot of dogs jumping on them to make puppies, we aren't quite sure. We always call our house dog Gorm. There's been a Gorm at Berg for fifty years. We knocked at the front door, but just then Auntie Ninna began to cough, and she had to bend double and spit, she coughed so hard. Fru Sten, the housekeeper, opened the door and she said, "Oh, dear! Oh dear! The doctor's out. Why didn't they send for him instead of letting you run through all that snow? It's an awful night. Only wolves should be out." Auntie Ninna had stopped coughing and she laughed and squeezed Fru Sten and said, "As if I wanted a doctor! It's only his gramophone I want. I'm ill with fun, but that's my only illness!" We wound up the gramophone in the dining room. It's an old one, but awfully smart, with red roses painted on the horn, and we put on the "Valse Brune" and waltzed off. Auntie Ninna sang, *"C'est la Valse Bru-ne, Chacun avec sa chacu-ne."* When we put on a fox-trot record I knew that the melody was exactly what

(*60*)

I'd felt like the whole day. I wanted to hop about, but Auntie Ninna showed me how to fox-trot and I learned it in a second. "I'm the gentleman," she said, and twirled her mustaches, walking up close to me. "May I have the honor, Fröken Jezza? Smile now, you idiot," she shouted at me. "Smile! Look sweet and womanly!" "How?" I asked. "Like this," she said, and opened her eyes enormously, seeming sort of amazed, then smiled a little and looked down and made her eyelashes flap up and down. "I could never learn all that," I said. "Let me be the gentleman instead. They needn't look anything in particular, need they?" Auntie Ninna laughed, and we grabbed each other and didn't care who was the gentleman or the lady. I stepped all over Auntie Ninna's feet, we laughed so that we had to fall down on the sofa, and each time we tried to get up we began to laugh again. We just couldn't move for laughter. Fru Sten came into the doorway and said, "Poor Doctor! I wish he could see you now, Fröken Ninna, beautiful as you are. His heart is sick from aching for you all these years. Yes, Fröken Ninna, sick and sore!" Just then we saw Doctor Borger's face pressed flat against the windowpane, and he came running in quickly, even though he is so fat, and threw his doctor's bag down on the chair. He really threw it down, he was so impatient to begin having fun! We were playing the "Valse Brune" on the gramophone again, and Auntie Ninna ran up to Doctor Borger and put his arm around her waist and began singing, *"C'est la Valse Bru-ne, Chacun avec sa chacu-ne,"* and they danced away. When the record ended, Doctor Borger opened the little corner cupboard and took out a bottle and poured out Malaga wine for all three of us, me too. We had two glasses each, and he kept staring at lovely Auntie Ninna, but she didn't do as he'd taught me and look womanly and sweet, she only laughed. When Doctor Borger learned that Auntie Ninna had run the whole way to his house in her little thin slippers, he got absolutely furious. Soon it was time to go, and he put us in his sleigh and got out a beautiful fur rug made of thirty red foxes that he has shot himself, with some of their tails on one side and some on the other. No wonder he's proud of it. Everyone knows he is the best shot in Berg after Uncle Rolf. The whole way home he kept his arm about Auntie Ninna's waist, which is as thin as the waist of a very gay wasp, and he never once looked at the road. His old horse was so clever he steered us home all by himself, and Doctor Borger didn't seem to mind that he took his good time about it. When we got upstairs, I asked Auntie Ninna, "Are you going to marry Doctor Borger?" "Marry him!" she screamed, and made a terrible face. "Marry that old sofa! I who am just crazy about good looks and melt at the sight of a handsome face!" I said, "Uncle Rolf's face, for instance? Do you melt at that?" "Oh, only about a hundred times a day," said Auntie Ninna. "But Uncle Rolf has no eyes for me. Perhaps his eyes are elsewhere already, though he doesn't realize it yet!" I don't know what Auntie Ninna meant by that. Then she laughed and squeezed me and said, "Soon they'll all be arriving for Christmas! The house is going to be chock-full. Oh, isn't it exciting? We will dance and dance and dance." She ran to her room laughing, and even after she'd closed the door I could still hear her singing, *"C'est la Valse Bru-ne, Chacun avec sa chacu-ne."*

14

Anna's Story

The day they all arrived, we put on our fine new clothes. For almost a month Fröken Rosa, the seamstress, has been tramping away on her sewing machine in the empty guest room. Those of us who never go to town, Jezza and I, and Frida, and Karna, get a new dress once a year from Fröken Rosa, who limps. The first of December the sleigh comes from Bo, and on top of it sits Fröken Rosa, clutching her darling Singer sewing machine. We all run out to meet her, even Gorm, the dog, who perhaps hopes that she'll make him a new coat in place of his old mangy one. Then Fröken Rosa is carried off to the guest room, which smells of apples and, after a while, of Fröken Rosa too. She brings such excitement with her! Everyone runs around giggling and chatting in her chemise and drawers, for we are all getting measured. Our dresses are almost the same each year. Karna and Frida get black woolen dresses, and I get a blue dress, the color of a thrush's eggshell. Jezza's dress is always red, from the reddest piece of material in Bo. Jezza laughs and hops about and hugs Fröken Rosa, so no wonder that Jezza and her terribly red dress are Fröken Rosa's favorites. Fröken Rosa keeps telling Jezza stories about all the exciting ladies in Bo. This year Jezza wanted her dress cut low and pinched in at the waist so as to look like those ladies. As Fröken Rosa snipped away at it, she whispered to Jezza that she'd made something just like it for someone called Mademoiselle Mitzi in Bo, whom Fröken Rosa says all the fine sea captains go to visit when they are in port. Aunt Emilia got all furious and Field Marshaly and told Fröken Rosa to shut up and to sew the dress together in front, but Jezza screamed at her, "If it's good enough for Mademoiselle Mitzi, then it's good enough for me!" Aunt Emilia, standing by the Singer sewing machine in nothing but her chemise and drawers, trembled like a leaf with fury and locked up Jezza in her clothes closet. After an hour she peeped in and asked Jezza if she would apologize, but Jezza was sitting on the floor and her eyes were black and she said, "I've spat on your coat and I've spat on your dresses and now I'm sitting here waiting for more spit so that I can spit on your hats." Anyhow, we were all very elegant when the big evening came, and at seven Karlson left for the station with the large sleigh, which has been repaired since the accident. The fine net that took Aunt Petronella ten years to crochet lay over Odin's and

Thor's haunches, and they were both so proud and kept throwing back their heads. Uncle Rolf, singing at the top of his lungs, drove in front of them in the little sleigh, hitched to his own mare, looking very elegant also with pine twigs stuck behind his ears. I lay on our window seat, thawing peepholes in the ice-coated pane with hot pennies, because otherwise we couldn't have looked out at all. We had just made four holes when they drove off, one for each of our four eyes, but it was fun making holes, so we kept on doing it, and there were a hundred holes, right over the whole windowpane, by the time we heard the bells coming back again. Auntie Ninna shouted from her room, "Here they are already! Good heavens! Jezza, come here quick and help me." We ran to her room, and it was her corset that she wanted help with, so we pulled and pulled at it till she was as thin as nothing at all, and she ran around and laughed and couldn't find anything and looked so sweet with her hair all brushed up in curls. She squeezed Jezza and said, "Stay with me, Jezza. Don't leave me for a moment. I'm feeling crazy, darling!" So Jezza stayed, and I went back to our room. I wished I needn't have gone down, but then they only would have called for me, and when I did come down, they'd all have noticed me much more. So I slipped in and stood behind Grandmother. There they all were, kissing and shouting to each other and laughing, and Karna was carrying around hot spiced wine. She had on her new Christmas dress and looked terribly elegant, and she giggled the whole time. She had probably sampled a lot of the *Glühwein* before carrying it in. Grandmother says that one ought always to drink heaps of hot wine before taking off one's overcoat after a long night drive. It makes the blood run around in one's stiff body. They looked like snowmen, standing about in their frozen fur coats. All my aunts were looking at Cousin Staffan and saying, "Heavens! Look at little Staffan. He has grown a mustache." I could just see how he hated it. Aunt Emilia, who is his mother, said, "You shave it off right away, you silly boy! Eighteen years old. Are you mad?" and Uncle Staffan said, "I tell you what, Emilia. I bet the kid is in love." They all laughed again in a horrid way. How I hate grown-up laughs! They are bad because they mean to hurt. Cousin Staffan went and stood near Grandmother, and I know why. Everyone wants to be close to Grandmother when he feels he is going to be attacked. Of course Uncle Staffan didn't notice anything, although Staffan is his own son, and he went on saying things that were just as hurtful as if he were walking over Staffan with heavy boots. "Why, the kid's begun writing love letters," he said in a loud ha-ha voice. "He scribbles love letters all day long to some fair lady. I wonder who she is. Won't you tell us, Staffan?" Oh, I was so sorry for Cousin Staffan! He grinned and pretended not to mind, only I knew that he did mind terribly. Just then we heard somebody come running down the stairs, and it was Auntie Ninna, with Jezza hopping along behind. Suddenly, though he hadn't said a word to me before, Cousin Staffan asked, "Do you still play with dolls, Anna? I suppose not." I didn't answer that stupid question, and I was sure he didn't care to know anyway. He had got red as a tomato when Auntie Ninna came down the stairs and he didn't even look at me but was staring terribly at her. Jezza called out, "Oh Auntie Ninna, look at Cousin Staffan! Isn't he beautiful? He has got a mustache and his hair is all shiny." Then everybody laughed again, except Pär and Gösta. They began to cry. They are like sponges, they have so much water in them. Grandmother said to me, "Put them to bed, Anna dear, Karna's busy." So I had to leave and take awful Pär and Gösta upstairs, just when everyone was so gay and happy. "It smells awful here in Berg," said Gösta on the way up. "A nasty dog or sausage smell or something." I was glad Jezza wasn't along, for I knew that she'd have smacked them hard for saying that. But just as I'd begun to undress them, she came running up to find me. We pulled off their boots and clothes, and of course they yelled and said we hurt them. Jezza said she hoped we did hurt them, idots who couldn't undress themselves though they were seven years old. "Wasn't Staffan's mustache beautiful?" she said to me, and I answered, "No," because Uncle Rolf doesn't wear a mustache. "Well, Auntie Ninna thought so anyhow," said Jezza. "I saw her kissing him on his mustache as I came up the staircase."

15

Jezza's Story

Everything is terrible now. It's Christmas, yet even so, everything is terrible. Anna and I didn't know that awful things could happen at Christmas, and what I've been thinking is that if awful things can happen at Christmas, then they might happen on our birthdays too, or on Midsummer Day, or any of the great days of the year. And I've thought even more. I wish I hadn't now, but of course I didn't know beforehand exactly what it was that I was going to think. I thought that if one can't be sure of the big special days, then one certainly can't be sure of any day. Tomorrow or the day after tomorrow, which sounds safe because it's so near, might turn out to be a terrible day! It all began at breakfast. We were seated around the table, talking about all the marvelous fun that was coming, and eating crackly Christmas ham, when Aunt Emilia, the Field

Marshal, ran in with the most terrible face, all twisted and not looking like a face at all. Her hair was still in long plaits and she had buttoned up her dress all wrong. "Mother!" she shrieked, meaning Grandmother, and then, "Rolf! Order the sleigh this minute," she said. Staffan and I are leaving, and we are taking young Staffan with us from this house of iniquity. Oh, I'm going crazy. This is going to be the end of me." Everybody ran up to her and there was terrible excitement. Even Gorm the Sixth got caught up in the hubbub and began to bark and jump around and nip everyone's legs. I thought the Field Marshall really was going crazy, as she said. She certainly looked crazy in the face. Well, in the end they made her go into the drawing room and shut the door, and Anna and I heard them all speaking and screaming in there, and we were sure that we heard both Aunt Emilia and Aunt Petronella weeping. Fancy their weeping, grown-up people, both of them! Of course, Pär and Gösta, who were outside with us, began to cry too. Those two sponges are always dripping! Even Cousin Gunhild, who's older than we are, wept a little. At last Grandmother came in to us, loking just the same as always. One could see that she hadn't been weeping, and she looked terribly calm. She told us, "Aunt Emilia has had a shock and it relieves her to act like that. It's nothing to worry about, only something to forget, dear children." She walked out into the hall and we all followed her, for we didn't know what else to do. "I'm a little tired," said Grandmother. "I'm going to sit by the window and look out at the snow. There's fresh snow since last night. You'd better run out of doors, all of you, this house isn't a good place just now." So we went and played in the barn and had fun. Altogether there were eight of us, and it's lovely to play games when you are eight instead of just two, as we usually are. We played "Pope" and a lot of other games, and we were four on each side. Anna kept hold of Pär and Gösta so they shouldn't fall over all the time, and she was wonderful the way she kept explaining to them about the games, explaining the same thing ten times over. When the gong boomed for lunch I thought that everything would be all right now and we were going to begin the Christmas celebrations. It wasn't all right, though. It was all wrong. We had our new dresses on, and we walked into the dining room, Grandmother first, but no one spoke or made jokes, and they all looked as if they'd been weeping and were going to weep again. When we were seated I could see that there were four places too many, although there were so many of us that it was difficult at first to see who wasn't there. Neither Aunt Emilia nor Uncle Staffan nor Cousin Staffan had come to lunch, nor had Auntie Ninna. "What's happened to Auntie Ninna?" I asked. "Is she ill?" Everyone looked at me as if I'd said something terrible. "Shut up, can't you!" said Uncle Rolf, and it was the first time I'd ever heard him talk to anybody angrily. If everything hadn't been so queer, I'm sure that would have made me want to cry too. We'd just begun on the wonderful Christmas *lutfisk*, that fish that has to lie about in different kinds of baths for weeks before Christmas and get all smelly and exciting, but it didn't taste very good after Uncle Rolf had told me to shut up. Aunt Petronella blew her nose, and her dress with all the bows down the front came undone, and then she wept some more. All at once Uncle Rolf pulled out his chair and said in a loud voice to Grandmother, "I'm going to bed and I'm going to stay there until this house is fit to live in again. All this sniveling gets me down." Uncle Rolf always goes to bed if anything happens that he doesn't like, such as people quarreling or the pipes leaking or other things like that. The two suckling pigs were carried in, looking so sweet with red apples in their mouths and fir twigs around their curly tails. The baked potatoes on the platter had red and yellow candles stuck into them, and all those candles were lit, yet even so nobody shouted "Hurrah! Hurrah!" as they always did at other Christmases. That was the most terrible thing of all, nobody shouting hurrah and applauding the pigs. It was then I began to think of how unsure everything was, even Christmas and lovely days. Now I'll never feel sure about anything again.

16

Anna's Story

We are forbidden to go to Auntie Ninna's room. Auntie Ninna doesn't come downstairs at all any longer, and when we ask them why, they say, "You wouldn't understand." "Explain it to us then," Jezza said the other day, but Aunt Petronella answered, "Oh, I couldn't do that! Oh! Oh!" and she got into her handkerchief and wept. Jezza says, "If they can't even explain, then they are stupider than we, who can't understand." This afternoon we sat in our room, thawing peepholes in the windowpane with hot pennies—not that there was very much to look at outside because it was three o'clock and it was already pitch dark. I'd just thawed out a little pattern of peepholes like a rose when Cousin Gunhild came in. "I know everything now," she said. "Your Aunt Ninna is a great sinner. She has committed a deadly sin with Cousin Staffan and she is

lost to God. Of course you're too young to understand. If Pastor Petrus heard about it, he might even
talk about her in church. Yes, he might!" Jezza has
always hated Cousin Gunhild. She has her hair done
up in curls so that nobody should see how straight
and straggly it is, and these holidays she has been
acting terribly grown-up because she has a new party
dress, a real lace one, and has learned to talk some
French. Well, after she'd said that about Auntie
Ninna, Jezza made a dash for her and she threw her
on the floor and bit her right in the cheek. Jezza
called out to me to help hold her, and we both sat on
her so that she couldn't get away. Pär and Gösta
helped too. "This will teach her," said Jezza. "This
will show her that we don't care what sniveling old
Pastor Petrus with his false teeth thinks, and we
don't care what Pastor Petrus' God thinks either.
When Grandfather was alive he despised Pastor
Petrus and that angry old God he's invented, who's
always pouncing on people and smiting them and
who lives in stuffy black churches, figuring out
whom He is to be angry with next. Everyone always
looks scared to death when he comes out of church
on Sunday after listening to Pastor Petrus talk of
God. But I suppose that God's especially angry with
you, Gunhild. That's why He put such awful stringy
hair on your head, just like a billy goat's beard!"
Jezza said that all quick, quick, and she was really
furious. Her eyes were black with fury. Cousin Gunhild tried to squirm away, but she couldn't with all

four of us sitting on her, especially as we were extra heavy from just having eaten lunch, with three huge helpings of stuffed pig each. "You're blaspheming!" Gunhild shouted. "Do you know what will happen to you for that? God might let the roof fall down on your heads and crush you!" "Of course He might," said Jezza. "I wouldn't be a bit surprised. He's always getting full of wrath and smiting someone. I wouldn't put it past Him to make the roof of Berg fall in." Then Cousin Gunhild said, "Well, anyway, your Aunt Ninna's scared of God and she's ashamed of the awful thing she's done. That's why she locks herself up in her room and never comes downstairs. She's ashamed, ashamed, ashamed of what she and Cousin Staffan did in bed. Cousin Staffan's going to get sent off to the navy and he won't touch land for three years, because otherwise he'd only come running back to Berg and sin some more. As to your Aunt Ninna, if she dared come downstairs, we'd all point our fingers at her and call out, 'Shame on you!'" Jezza smacked Cousin Gunhild in the face and said, "Nobody as lovely as Auntie Ninna need ever be ashamed to come downstairs. Ugly people might be ashamed to show themselves and their stringy hair, but not beautiful people like Auntie Ninna." Then she said to me, "What should we do with her? Should we bite her some more?" "No," I said. "It wouldn't do any good. It wouldn't make her any less awful." Jezza thought a moment and whispered to me, "Let's run out and lock her in." I whispered it to Pär and Gösta, but I had to repeat it twice before they understood. Their brains must be made of wood. Suddenly we all jumped up and ran out of the room and locked the door. Jezza and I went to my staircase. I was so full of cry I could hardly keep it down any more, and Jezza was too. She said, "Oh, I must cry now. It's coming." She began to cry and then I cried too. We cried until the clock struck four and we heard Frida or someone laying the table in the dining room for afternoon coffee. We moved up to the top step then, where it is dark and nobody can see you, and began to cry again. Before, whenever we have had to cry about something, we've cried and bit, and then it was all over, but this time it wasn't over at all. It hurt to cry, it was like a real ache, because we weren't crying about just one thing, we were crying about every-thing. Jezza said, "Let's kiss," and we kissed and kissed, but even that didn't help. Luckily Jezza got the hiccups and after that it was a little better. She said, "They never tell us anything. Here they go and spoil the whole Christmas, so that it doesn't even smell like Christmas in the house any longer, and they won't let us know why they did it. When they're happy about something we have to be happy too, when they're sad we have to be sad, but we mayn't even know why we are to be one or the other. I wish we knew everything and could decide for our-selves if we wanted to be sad or happy, and if things that happened were bad or good. I've stopped believing in all of them. From now on I've got to find out everything for myself." I loved Jezza awfully and I squeezed her hard. Jezza is always so terribly something, terribly angry or terribly gay or terribly sad, anyhow always terribly something, and that is lovely. "Should I tell you everything that I find out?" she asked me. "I'm going to travel away and find out everything, and I'm sure it's going to be all different from what they've told us. I'm going to find out what's sad and what isn't and what's bad and what isn't, and after I've found out everything I'll come home to Berg and tell you." I said to Jezza, "Meanwhile I'll be finding out everything right here because I am never going to leave Berg. And I'll tell you what I've found out too." We sat there for a little while more and before we left, Jezza told me something lovely. She said, "I like being here on your stairs. It feels a little like Grandmother's room."

17

Jezza's Story

I was sitting in the kitchen with my feet on the stove, thawing them out a bit after shoveling snow. Frida and Fru Boberg were counting laundry in the passage for Fru Boberg to wash, and Fru Boberg said, "Is it true what they say, that his own mother found him in Fröken Ninna's bed?" Frida clacked with her tongue and said, "So it's already out in the village, is it? Gracious! Gracious! Gracious! Well, seeing that you've heard, I might as well tell you just what happened. She went to his room with his gift on Christmas morning, a pair of black silk suspenders with mauve stripes, very elegant, with his initials embroidered on them in mauve. She'd showed them to me the night before and I'd had a feel of the silk. It's only in the capital that they wear such fine suspenders, but of course nothing was ever too good for Master Staffan. He's the apple of his mother's eye. Well, she didn't find him in his room, and his bed hadn't been slept in either, so then she ran to every room in the house to look for him and to ask if anyone had seen him, and to her sister's, Fröken Ninna's, room as well. There they were, sound asleep in Fröken Ninna's big bed! I suppose he'd meant to go back to his own room afterwards, but fell asleep. Well, no wonder his mother took on so. He's only eighteen; he was eighteen the twenty-third of last November. I remember all the grandchildren's birthdays and all my own nieces' children's birthdays and nearly everyone else's birthday, too. Why, do you know that I've got more than a hundred birthdays in my head, and I never get two of them mixed up?" That was true. Frida does manage to keep track of everybody's birthday, and usually surprises the person with a picture postcard with a heart on it. Fru Boberg had been listening to her without once interrupting, and she didn't interrupt now either, but I was so curious that I had to call out from the kitchen, "But what had they done that was so terrible, Frida? Had Auntie Ninna stolen something, or what?" Frida howled as if I'd stuck a pin in her. "Bless my soul!" she shrieked. "The wicked child's been listening to everything in the kitchen. How much did you hear?" she asked me. "Not much," I said. "Only about Aunt Emilia's coming in and finding them sound asleep. But you didn't say what had happened." "Bless the child," said Fru Boberg. "Now run away and play and

forget all about it." That was my day to read
Uncle Rolf to sleep after lunch. As soon as the
meal was over, I went to get the newspaper and
squatted down near the fire in his bedroom, because
they'd made me leave the kitchen stove before my
feet had finished thawing out. On the first page in
big headlines was written "Splendor of the English
coronation." "No, spare me that drivel," said Uncle
Rolf when I began to read about it. "Read something else instead, but don't read too loud. What's
the point of your reading to me if it keeps me awake?
There's nothing but lies in the papers anyhow." So
I turned to the weather forecast instead, where it
said, "Steady fall in temperature, sharp northeast
winds, local snowfalls." I tried to listen to the wind
to see if they had lied about its being northeasterly,
but the logs in the fireplace were making such a
noise I couldn't hear a thing. The logs are full of
sap, and they keep hissing and spitting out scum.
Seeing that the newspapers are always full of lies,
I think it's funny people ever buy one and spend ten
whole öre for it, which I take a whole morning and
afternoon to earn shoveling snow. Perhaps the main
reason people buy newspapers is to get themselves
to sleep, like Uncle Rolf, or to wrap up parcels with
or to use in the toilet when the other paper gives out.
When I'd finished the weather forecast, I read about
a new bridge, and then there didn't seem to be anything else to read about except the splendors of the
English coronation, and as Uncle Rolf was breathing

awfully hard, I supposed that he was asleep and that
he wouldn't care much what I read, as long as I read
something, for it wakes him up when I stop reading.
My, but that coronation was elegant! That King
George the Fifth is certainly the luckiest fellow. He
had six gray horses to pull him—I don't know why,
but that's what the paper said. I thought that perhaps he was terribly fat, like Doctor Borger, and
that was why he needed six, but when I came to think
of it, Doctor Borger's one horse manages to pull him
quite all right, especially as the doctor gets out as
soon as they come to a hill, he is so kind-hearted.
Perhaps the King wouldn't care to do that, especially
not at his coronation, when he's all dressed up and
terribly elegant in his long red robes, like a lady.
Perhaps he needs six horses because there are a lot
of steep hills in London. The King made a lovely
speech. He did say one terrible lie though, a real
newspaper lie. He said that he'd do anything in his
power to ease the burden of his people. Why, even
I could see through that! I know the King has heaps
and heaps of money and a table service of real gold.
Frida says that if he sold only one plate, a hundred
of his hungriest people could eat for a whole year.
But he doesn't sell a thing, he hangs onto his plates
like dear life, and he has even got soldiers with
bayonets standing around his palace to see that nobody gets in to steal a single plate. Uncle Rolf gave
a terrible snore. I looked at him. He'd pulled the
sheepskin rug that used to lie at the foot of his bed

right over him, because he's given his eiderdown
and nearly all his blankets to his tramps. Uncle Rolf
certainly is different from that King George the
Fifth! He's given away most of his clothes too, and
even the furniture in the office, all except the sofa.
The aunts are furious and wail that soon he'll begin
emptying the rest of the house, but he only laughs
at them and says a happy man needs practically nothing, just one pair of pants and a bed. Well, in the
end it got awfully boring reading, so I stopped and
began to think of what Frida and Fru Boberg had
said about Auntie Ninna. I forgot that Uncle Rolf
was trying to fall asleep, and I said, "Why did Aunt
Emilia take on so because Cousin Staffan slept in
Auntie Ninna's bed?" Uncle Rolf said, "O-o-o!"
and woke right up. "What's this?" he said. "What
the devil!" I don't know why he acted so excited all
at once. He thought a moment, and then he said,
"Well, seeing that you want to know, I'll tell you
why, very young Jezza. Because Aunt Emilia's a
pin-brained old hen and has the usual idea that a
lady and a gentleman shouldn't sleep in the same
bed before Pastor Petrus or some other black frog
of a minister has given his permission. Or if they do
sleep together they ought to wake up in time. That's
an important thing to remember for your education,
Jezza, and one that your governess isn't apt to mention. Always try to wake up in time! Well, go on
and read now, for the love of God." He turned over
and pulled the sheepskin above his head, and I read

on and on in that old newspaper. I fell asleep myself
and dreamed that I was in bed with Cousin Staffan
and he was covered with hair, and when I woke up I
found that my own hair had fallen over my face.

18

Anna's Story

I hadn't seen the wild duck, Hanna, for two days. She hadn't come into the chicken coop or into the yard behind the barn, and yesterday morning when Karlson went to feed the horses, he found her frozen fast in the pond. It was five o'clock, and black, without a star in the sky, but just then one star did come out to help poor Hanna, who'd been sending out special prayers saying that she was about to die and please, would a star come out and shine on her so that somebody would see her and do something about it. The carp in the pond don't mind being frozen over, for they stick their heads in the mud and let their tails freeze fast and can stay like that till spring. Of course they taste terrible in spring after having sat in the mud all winter, and Frida has to rub them with lemon to take away the mud taste before Uncle Rolf will eat them with wine sauce.

But Hanna isn't a carp, she's only a duck. Well, when Karlson looked over the pond, he saw something that looked like a bent twig, and it turned out to be poor Hanna's neck and head lying flat on the ice. That was all of her that he could see. Karlson ran to the stable to fetch his axe and then he ran all the way back. It was nice of him to run like that, especially with that bad leg of his that got mixed up once in the thrashing machine. He said himself that it was rather nice of him to hurry so. Karlson walked out on the pond with his axe and began to chop the ice around Hanna, but she didn't open an eye. He chopped out a big block of ice with Hanna sitting cooped up, half dead, inside, and carried it to the kitchen. Then they fetched me, because I was the one who'd fed her and made her feel welcome in Berg when the other wild ducks went south last autumn and she was too old to go along. She is such a good duck, and it was awful to see her body inside the block of ice, with her head hanging out like a dead tulip on its stalk. When I looked at her I knew she reminded me of something that was sadder still, and I tried not to remember what it was. I tried, but it wasn't any use. It came to me suddenly. She was just like Auntie Ninna lying on her sofa last night when we went to her room against the aunts' orders. Auntie Ninna had been lying sleeping, and her book had fallen to the floor and her darling, sweet head had slipped off the cushion and lay sideways, looking so terribly tired. Her neck had looked like a beauti-

ful flower stalk, and that's why the wild duck reminded me of her. I began to weep, and of course
they thought it was because of Hanna I was weeping. I let them think so. That just shows how easy it
is to cry for one thing and let people think you're
crying for something else! I'd never thought of doing it before. Hanna soon got melted out, and we
wrapped her in warm cotton and gave her a drink
of brandy, and then she went to sleep on the stove
happily. They all expected me to be gay again, so I
pretended that I was, but that ache I've had for two
whole weeks, ever since Christmas, was there all the
time. I hadn't cried since that one time with Jezza
on the stairs, but I felt that there was still a lot of
cry in me. I couldn't cry any more about the duck,
who was alive and had even opened one eye and
winked at me, so I had to leave the kitchen to look
for another place to do it. The door of Grandmother's room was open, and that was a good thing
because my cry was coming on so quickly it was almost there. I ran into Grandmother's room and
right into her lap, and I cried and cried and cried.
She didn't ask me why I was crying—she never asks
a single question, so that's why I told her. I said,
"Berg is full of wicked people. I never knew it,
I thought we were all good. We're all so wicked
that Auntie Ninna doesn't dare come downstairs and
nobody but you and Uncle Rolf go up to see her.
She looked all gray yesterday and she's going to get
ill as anything. She can't stand being hated so! When

everybody left to go back to town, they didn't even go up to say good-bye to her. It's terrible, the way everything has got since Christmas. Everyone's whispering and whispering, Frida and Karna and everyone, and today when Fru Boberg and Gudrun were milking their cows they were saying something to each other and stopped quickly when they saw me. Everyone in Berg has become nasty." Grandmother closed her eyes and leaned her head back on her chair. After a moment she said to me, "Should I tell you a story? It's about a man who had a beautiful garden. Such a beautiful garden it was! A clear stream ran through it with orange trees growing on its banks. Thick white blossoms grew on the orange trees, and later on they were heavy with ripe yellow fruit. The flowers in the grass sparkled like butterflies. All around this precious garden was a wall, and the wall had two gates, one leading to the country, the other to the town. But something very sad happened, little Anna. The man loved his garden, but he was thoughtless and careless, and he had poor judgment. Day and night he left the gates of his garden wide open, so that people got in the habit of walking through the one gate and out through the other. There was no harm in that, he thought. But soon the people began to linger on their way. They sat down for a while, built fires, even had their picnics there. They trod on the flowers, threw refuse in the river, and left much litter behind when they finally went away. The owner grew worried at last and decided to close the gates, but in the course of the years they had fallen off or been stolen. It was too late. The garden was ruined. It had become nothing but a common thoroughfare, a place for litter and for junk." When Grandmother got through with her story, I said to her, "Poor man, Grandmother!" and she answered, "Poor you, Anna! Poor you and poor Jezza! You are that man and your mind is that garden and your ears those two wide-open doors. You never close them but let Frida leave her rubbish, and Cousin Gunhild leave *her* rubbish, and everybody leave some trash. When you are a grown woman, your mind will be like most other people's minds, a common thoroughfare littered with rubbish. The clear stream that once flowed inside you will be all clogged up." She stopped speaking and her eyes looked far away. I put my head under her shawl, and then I had to cry again, because it was so terrible to think of my mind being that garden. Grandmother's blouse smelled of sweet warm roses. She kissed me a long time, much longer than usual, and said, "It need never happen, Anna. It won't happen if you do not wish it, but right now is the time to lock up your precious garden."

19

Jezza's Story

We were cleaning up under Apollo. I think a donkey smells worse than any horse, and Apollo is the worst-smelling donkey in the world, but Anna doesn't think so. The most dreadful thing happened. I saw the sleigh coming up the driveway with Karlson driving, and caught sight of a big black hat with a green pompon. I shouted to Anna, and she had time to see that awful pompon before the sleigh turned the corner. We looked at each other. "It can't be the tenth of January already," said Anna. "It just can't be." "Let's run away and hide," I told her. "No," said Anna. "It's too cold. We'd freeze off an ear, like Karlson's brother did during the winter maneuvers. It looked horrible, his head where the ear had been." I said, "It looked horrible because Karlson's brother is a man, and he has no hair to cover up the spot. It wouldn't even show on us."

"I want both my ears all the same," said Anna. As we were talking, the sleigh drove up, with our awful governess, Fröken de Bar, sitting inside. It was too late to run away then. She'd seen us. She called out, "Good morning, Anna! Good morning, Jezza!" Oh, it was certainly her all right. Everyone else in Berg, even our aunts and uncles, talk naturally, and it was awful to have to hear Fröken de Bar's terribly elegant way of speaking again. We walked toward her slowly, holding each other around the waist for help, and when we got quite close, Karlson turned his head and winked at us. Fröken de Bar kissed us in her dreadful way. It's mostly her big nose one feels when she kisses. She pretended to smile, but she doesn't know how to. No one ever smiles at her, because she's so haughty and queenly, so perhaps she's never seen what a real smile looks like. I was so furious with her for making it be the tenth of January when I thought it was only the eighth, that I said, "Oh, how red your nose is! You must be frozen. Your nose is terribly red, especially the tip." Her eyes, which always pop out, popped out some more, and she said, "Ugh! You two look like hooligans. You smell, too. What have you been doing?" "Cleaning out dung," I answered. "Donkey dung, Fröken de Bar." Karlson howled with laughter, and she gave him *such* a look, but he was driving off already, swinging his whip and laughing like anything. Darling old Karlson! Fröken de Bar took us by the shoulders and led us into the hall. "Get washed up

and brushed up right away," she said, "and get your
school books ready. We'll begin our Latin lesson as
soon as I've unpacked. What a state you've got into
over the holidays!" We were just walking away
when Fröken de Bar said, "What's all this about
your poor Aunt Ninna? I hear that she doesn't leave
her room." I felt Anna's leg nudging mine. She's always so scared I'll say something that I shouldn't.
I was careful. I said, "Auntie Ninna isn't poor. She's
prettier and more elegant and lovelier than anyone." Fröken de Bar didn't let me finish. She closed
her long purple eyelids slowly, just as if she were
pulling blinds down over her eyes, and she looked
at me out of the cracks haughtily. "That just shows
how few real ladies you have seen, my poor child!
It just shows." "Well, Staffan thinks she's beautiful
anyway," I said, "and Uncle Rolf thinks so too. He
told me so." Fröken de Bar's nose got all red again.
It looked as if it ached. She sucked her lips until
they got thin, thin, and then she said, "Please spare
me further confidences. I don't believe a word you
say. Your Uncle Rolf is a man of the world, while
your aunt, your aunt . . ." Fröken de Bar couldn't
even finish her sentence her nose ached so badly,
I suppose. Her nostrils opened and shut as if she
were smelling something bad, and she stalked out
of the room with her long neck stuck out before her,
looking like the camel in the picture in the hallway,
only sillier. We ran to Frida, who always hates
everyone we hate, and Frida said, "What's she doing

here today? Why, it's only the eighth and she isn't
supposed to come until the tenth. She can't keep
away from Berg, or from someone in Berg, I ought
to say. Why she comes bothering us at all I don't
see. Can't you two girls read and spell yet?" "Of
course," I said, "but there are a lot of other things
one has to learn." "Hmmm," said Frida. "If there
are, it's not Fröken de Bar that can teach you. What
does she know of anything? She's never done an
honest day's work in her life, sweating away from six
in the morning till midnight, as I do. Why, your
Uncle Rolf's tramps could teach you more useful
things than she!" Then we told Frida what Fröken
de Bar had said, and about her stalking out of the
room like a camel. Frida laughed so hard that she had
to go out of doors and blow her nose in the snow.
She said, "She's sweet on your Uncle Rolf and has
been for years, that old camel of yours. There's not
a woman who doesn't fall for him," I said. "You're
sweet on Uncle Rolf too, aren't you, Frida? I'd much
rather have you marry him than she, only I suppose
you can't because you're so old and you're a servant."
Frida said, "Well, I am a servant and I'm proud of
it because I am a good servant. I'm a first-rate cook
—almost a chef, one might say. Fröken de Bar is
only a servant too, when it comes to that. She's paid
to teach, just as I'm paid to cook. She hasn't a penny
to her name, and no one to support her but that old
souse of a colonel, her father, who got kicked out of
the army on account of his drinking. If she dares

wink an eye at your Uncle Rolf I'll put rat poison in her tea, that I will, and you can ask the storeroom rats if it's a belly-ache or something worse they get from the stuff I cook up for them. You can ask, I say, but the fact is there aren't any of them alive to tell you."

20

Anna's Story

Yesterday Karlson's wife had twins. My, Karlson was sad! That makes ten. He's like me, he gets new ones all the time, only mine don't eat and his do. That's why he's so sad about it. Jezza and I are sad too, because now Berta and Alfhild will have to stay at home and look after that new pair, and they won't be able to come to the house and play. We'll still have Thyra though, and except when she becomes "Friday Thyra," we like her too. Thyra's father is the baker, and Friday is the day when they bake bread. We always keep forgetting how near Friday is, but on Thursday, while we're playing, Thyra suddenly gets a funny look on her face and says, "Tomorrow is Friday. I'll have to stay in the bakery and help them with the bread." She gets all grown-up and different and important then. Her face gets like Frida's or Karna's after they've been playing with us for a while and say, "Now I must get back to my work." We feel snubbed and young and left out of things. Thyra isn't older than we, but she gets the same sort of face when she talks about Friday, for she knows that on Friday she does real work, helping her father and mother in the bakery, and she knows that we know it and that we feel sort of silly, not having any work to do. Each time after she's said it, we all three begin to act differently and pretty soon she goes away. Then next day is Friday, and Jezza and I know that Thyra's having an important day in the bakery with the others, brushing the loose flour off the loaves as they come out of the oven, and wrapping them and delivering them in the village. When she comes back on Saturday, everything's all right again, and it is a whole week before the next baking day. But it's funny how soon it gets to be Thursday and the whole thing starts over again! Last week Thyra said, "It's my grandma's birthday tomorrow. My mother's baking a cake, and if your aunts will let you come, she'd be pleased to have you for coffee at two o'clock." We *were* glad! We aren't asked out terribly much in Berg. We once went to tea a year ago when Doctor Borger's mother came to visit him, but that was the last time. Well, next day after lunch we went off to the party, and we ran the whole way, because Jezza couldn't wait for the fun to begin. We got there at twenty past one. I thought it was too early to go in, but Jezza said no. She said that

twenty past one was going on for two and that it
would be terrible fun to help brush the bread, like
Thyra does on Fridays. So we went in. Thyra's
grandmother and Thyra's mother and Thyra all
came out of the kitchen, and they quickly shut the door
behind them. They were dressed awfully fine. They
said, "How do you do, Fröken Jezza?" and dropped
a curtsy, and "How do you do, Fröken Anna?" and
dropped a curtsy to me. We said, "How do you do?"
and then we all just stood there. Even Thyra didn't
say anything more to us. She had on her best pink
dress and looked terribly "Friday Thyra," and she
was so polite to Jezza and me, just as if we hadn't
met every day since I don't know when. Jezza said,
"We're a little bit early. I'd love to brush off bread
or have some fun in the bake house. May we,
Thyra?" Thyra looked upset, as if Jezza had said
just the wrong thing. She and her grandmother and
mother all looked at each other and said, "Oh, no,
of course not, Fröken Jezza." Then they took us into
the best room and said, "Sit down, please!" and they
all three went out of the room. We sat on two chairs,
with a table with a little pine tree in a pot right between us. We couldn't see each other because of that
pine. It smelled queer in the best room, not a smell
of apples, nor of soap, but of something like them,
and it was terribly hot and almost dark. The blinds
were halfway down. There was a clock with little
bronze children around it. It struck twice, for half
past one. We didn't know if we could move, or if

they might come in just then, so we stayed where we were. Then it struck three times. That was for a quarter to two. I was getting so sleepy, but just as it struck two, the door opened and Thyra carried in a tray with cups, and a coffeepot with a golden lid. Her mother carried in a China platter with holes all around the edge and a red ribbon going in and out of the holes and tying in a bow. The cake lay in the middle with whipped cream on top. Thyra's mother said, "If you please, young ladies!" and we got up and went over to the table. An enormous yawn came into my mouth, but I bit into it so as to stop it from coming out whole and it only came out in tiny puffs that nobody noticed. We stood and waited for Thyra's grandmother and mother to sit down, but in the end we saw that they were waiting for us to do it. That felt queer. We didn't know what to do. Thyra said, "Please sit down." Then we sat down and Thyra poured out the coffee and cut big chunks of cake for us. There were only three cups. Jezza said to Thyra, "Aren't your mother and grandmother having anything, Thyra?" "Oh, no," answered Thyra's mother. "We'll have ours later in the kitchen." Then she turned to Thyra's grandmother and said, "Come, Grandma," and began pulling her out of the room. The grandma didn't want to go, but Thyra's mother coaxed her along. They got her out all right, but she was back again almost at once, at least her face was, sticking through the crack of the door. I thought she wanted to watch

(*97*)

us and see that we didn't eat up all her birthday cake. I'd have done it too, but that wasn't why she was looking at us at all. She never looked at the cake but kept staring at us and smiling and nodding. Goodness knows what she saw to look at, but she seemed to be having a nice time. Thyra was quite different from usual. She wouldn't talk or laugh but only kept pouring coffee and cutting cake, and I couldn't reach Jezza's leg with mine to ask, "Why is she like that?" I was full of cake right up to my mouth. I was stuffed with it. Thyra got up and said, "Excuse me." Imagine her saying that to us! Then she began to clear away. I'd never seen her look so "Friday Thyra." Jezza said, "We'll help you," and got up, but Thyra shouted, "Oh no, no! Sit down, please! Sit down." So we had to sit down again, though we had been doing nothing but sit and sit. Thyra carried everything out and stayed away I don't know how long. It kept getting hotter and hotter in there, and it smelled coffee now as well as that other queer smell. It had struck three by the time Thyra came back. "What would you like to do now?" she said. Jezza said, "I'd like best to brush bread or do something in the bake house. Where is it?" Thyra looked all upset again and said, "Oh, but you can't!" "Why?" asked Jezza. "Because we are having a party," said Thyra. "Besides, the bake house isn't meant for playing in. It must be kept just so. We can't have it getting all messed up." "I wasn't going to mess it up," said Jezza. "Why should I mess it up?" "I don't know," answered Thyra, "but the kitchen in Berg always looks a sight after your aunts have been down to make a dish. Frida says that it takes her an hour to clear up afterwards and it takes her almost another hour before they come, getting everything ready for them and cutting and peeling the food. Ladies don't know how to do anything themselves." Thyra sounded so angry. I think she was angry because of Jezza's not really understanding that this was an elegant party. And then it was so hot in there! It would have been easy for anybody to get angry. Jezza said, "It isn't true! My aunts know how to work as well as you. Why, they're always busy. They're busy all day long." Thyra said, "Busy doing nothing! They don't work, ladies never do. They just play at working to make the time pass." Jezza shouted, "You just say that because you're envious!" Thyra got all red in the face. She said, "Envious! As if I'd ever want to be a lady! A silly goose who gets tired all the time and can't do anything except read or do some knitting or have headaches. As if I'd ever want to be idle and count the laundry for someone else to wash, and always have someone else do my real work for me! No, thank you!" I didn't want Jezza to answer, so I asked, "What *do* you want to do when you grow up, Thyra?" She said, "I want to work. I want to bake bread and sell it, like my mother and grandmother, and take care of my children and make my husband's dinner and clean my house and work in my garden and darn our clothes and scrub. I want to work until I'm as old as my grandma." I said to Thyra, "That's exactly what I want to do too!" but Jezza was terribly angry mainly at not being allowed to go to the bake house, which she'd looked forward to doing. I didn't want Jezza and Thyra to quarrel. Bad things you don't really mean deep down jump out awfully easily when you quarrel. Those bad things don't live in the heart—they must live somewhere in the neck, they jump out so quickly. I said, "Should we play dolls, Thyra?" She said, "Oh yes!" and sounded really glad that now she didn't have to have a quarrel. Of course she and Jezza do like each other awfully. I said to her, "Go and get them from your room and we'll begin," but Thyra answered, "I haven't got a room. I sleep in the same bed with Grandma. Anyway, we couldn't play with my ordinary dolls in here in the best room, especially not at a party." She got out a white box from the cupboard and took out the doll Grandmother gave her two years ago. The doll looked just the same as it had then, with crinkly curls and a pink silk dress and silly feet with shoes and socks painted on. She looked like a lady, I thought, like one of those idiot ladies Thyra had talked about who can't do any proper work. I was the mother, Jezza the maid, and Thyra was the father. But it wasn't any fun at all. If I wanted the doll to sit down or to lie down, Thyra called out, "Oh, don't do that. You're going to crease her dress." We walked round and round the table, taking the doll for walks. Jezza and I almost fell asleep. At five o'clock someone knocked at the front door and it was Karna, come to fetch us, because Aunt Emilia, the Field Marshal, had said that we oughtn't to walk home alone in the dark. We went almost crazy with joy. We'd begun to think that we'd never get out of that awful room again. We ran into the hall, almost knocking each other down, and stepping on each other's feet. "Am I too early?" Karna said. "Oh no, Karna, not at all," we shouted, and squeezed her and kissed her, and we got into our overshoes as quick as anything and said good-bye and thanks to Thyra's mother and grandmother. They wiped their fingers before shaking hands with us. Then we rushed out, we were so scared they might try to stop us. It was lovely on the road, so cold and icy, and we ran around and shouted and danced and jumped. Jezza said, "Karna, is it true that ladies aren't like real women?" "I don't know," said Karna. Jezza said, "They're not real women because they're silly and messy and keep getting tired and nervous and can't do anything properly and always have to have someone else do all the hard work for them." Karna said, "Well, that's true, that is. That's certainly true," but then she said quickly, "Whom have you heard all that nonsense from, Fröken Jezza?" Jezza grabbed hold of Karna's sleeve and made her stop in the road, and said, "Look at us, Karna! We aren't ladies any more, Anna or I. We'll never be ladies as long as we live."

Karna looked really scared and said, "I don't know what's come over you, Fröken Jezza, to talk like that. It's very nice and lovely to be a lady, I'm sure." Jezza said, "Oh, no, it isn't. When we grow up, Anna is going to wash her own children and get dinner for her husband, and I'm going to be a writer and work hard and earn money. It isn't nice to be a lady, it's silly and awful. Do you hear, Karna? Terribly silly and absolutely *awful*!"

21

Jezza's Story

On Sunday we were sliding down the banister when Fröken de Bar stalked through the hall. She looked like a silly queen in her long flowing black coat with high neck and lace ruffles, which she likes to wear to show off her distinguished looks. Her hat with the green pompon was sitting right on top of her hair, like queens' hats do. She didn't see us because she was busy stuffing pink cotton wool into her ears, as she always does before going out in the cold. Then, when she comes in, she can't hear a thing and keeps saying, "What? What? Speak properly, please!" "Your cotton wool, Fröken de Bar," we shout at her. "I beg your pardon?" "Cotton wool!" we howl and point at her ears. Then she gets furious and fishes it out with her long, long fingers that she's so proud of because they are white, and long as pencils, with the nails for sharp awful points. Fröken de Bar walked through the hall and closed the front door behind her and marched down the front steps. Anna and I didn't have a thing to do and we had slid on the banister until we were sore. I said, "I suppose she is off to church. I wonder if it's any fun and what it's really like there. Let's follow her and just have a peep inside." In one way it's a pity that they don't let us go to church, because that would give us something to do on Sunday morning, but Grandfather used to be against churchgoing because pastors preach one way and live another, which is called hypocrisy, and Grandmother says that is crime number one. Well, Fröken de Bar trotted along with her tiny steps. Her legs are like sticks, and one can't believe that there are knees in the middle that really bend. The bells had finished ringing and that meant she was late, but she had to walk ladylike all the same, though there wasn't even a horse out to look at her. I had put on Auntie Ninna's lambskin jacket, which had been hanging in the hall, because I was sure Auntie Ninna wouldn't mind my using her jacket, now that she stays in her room all day. It smelled violet from her bottle called "Amour-Amour," the one with the picture of the lady and the gentleman in evening clothes looking at each other. The sleeves were so long that my hands were just nowhere, and I couldn't even scratch myself. It's lucky Fröken de Bar had those bits of cotton in her ears so she didn't hear us walking behind her, but just as we came to church she turned about and saw us. "What's this?"

she said. "Anna! Jezza! And what have you got on? You look terrible!" The church door opened before she finished talking, and the organ boomed out at us like thunder, angry and loud. We could see that there weren't many people inside, but it looked as if there might be some fun in there all the same. "Can we come with you, Fröken de Bar?" I asked. She said, "Certainly not! You know very well that your grandfather never wanted any of his household to go to church." I said, "But just this once, Fröken de Bar! We've never been inside in our lives and I'm sure that Pastor Petrus can't do us any harm if we go just once." "Ssh!" said Fröken de Bar. "Are you crazy? What would people think if they heard you? Run home, both of you, this minute." We had to hop aside, for just then Herr Ren, the store-keeper, came dashing around the corner in his sleigh. "Here's a surprise!" he said when he'd jumped out. "The two young ladies from Berg! Coming to church, are you? Hurry in. It's no weather for dawdling, my honored ladies. It's thirty below zero!" He held the door open for us, and Fröken de Bar didn't know what to do. We slipped past her before she had time to think, and her long nose twitched, she was so nervous and so ashamed of the way we looked. At first we sat down on the wrong side of the aisle, with the men, and we had to move and slip over to the other side, right next to Fröken de Bar. It's funny that our church should be just like a cow stable, with cows on one side and bulls and

oxen on the other. I wonder why they have it ar-
ranged like that. In a stable it's because the bulls
want to jump on the cows all the time, but it can't
be for the same reason in a church. Fröken de Bar
began to sing from her hymnbook, and I sang too,
louder than anyone. The tune was nice, but it was
slow, so I changed the time, trying to make it sound
a bit more hoppy. I got so interested in singing that
I almost missed something. I would have if Anna
hadn't grabbed hold of my arm and pointed at Pastor
Petrus' face lying on the edge of that box-thing that
a little winding staircase leads up to. There his face
lay, with closed eyelids, looking like a big peeled
egg. I began to laugh but Fröken de Bar said, "Ssh!
Ssh!" and stepped on my foot. Anna grabbed my
arm again and said, "Why don't you look when
you're here for once?" I looked, and now he had
popped up, all of him. He was dressed in a black
coat and a black sort of cape, and there was a little
white starched something sticking out beneath his
chin. He was reading out of a big book; I think it
was the Bible. Grandmother says that the Bible is the
loveliest book of all but that nobody reads it much
because most parsons make it all sound so boring that
people yawn when they just hear the word "Bible."
It's true, for they were all yawning now, both in the
men's stalls and in the women's, where we sat. They
didn't even put their hands before their mouths, as
Fröken de Bar keeps after us to do. I looked at Pastor Petrus while he read and I thought if he had

been a Last Viking, as Grandfather was, he certainly would have had to kill himself long ago because of his looks. After he had read, he began to talk. It was a pity we couldn't hear what he said, for Anna and I have always wondered what they found to talk about in church every Sunday the whole year round. There must have been something the matter with his voice. First it wheezed, then it gave a loud squeak, and then it sank away altogether. His false teeth kept coming unhooked, and he had to suck them back into place. I asked Anna if she heard anything and she answered, "Yes, a word now and then, but nothing that hangs together." No one else could hear him either. They all began to cough and to scrape their feet, and the lady behind us blew her nose so loud that Anna and I gave a jump. Everybody tittered, but Pastor Petrus didn't notice a thing. I suppose he's deaf. He only talked on and on. Then suddenly everyone hopped up. I thought something had happened, a fire or something, but everything was all right. Fröken de Bar poked us to make us stand up too, but as soon as we had got up, everyone flopped down again. We began to laugh. Fröken de Bar said, "Ssh!" and looked furious. Then Pastor Petrus talked some more and drank a lot of water or something out of a pitcher. He must have remembered to take along something to drink when he climbed up into the box. That was clever of him, for of course everyone's thirsty on Sunday morning after having been drunk Saturday night. Suddenly all the people hopped up again, we too. That part of it, the hopping up, was fun. Then they sang, and it began to get awfully cold because someone had opened the door of the church. Pastor Petrus had dived out of sight, but pretty soon we saw him creeping along up in front where there were some candlesticks and flowers. I couldn't quite see what he was doing, for everyone was taller than me, but he looked as if he might be snipping off some of the dead flowers. That's a good thing to do, it makes the other flowers grow. When he had finished, we all marched out of the church, and I waved hello to the organist, but he didn't wave back. When we were outside, I asked Fröken de Bar, "What did he talk about? Why didn't anybody listen?" She said, "They did listen, you naughty child." I said, "They did not! They kept yawning and looking at us. What did he find to talk about the whole time anyway?" "Not talk, preach," Fröken de Bar answered. "He preached about doing right, and about God, which are two things you know nothing of." I said, "When I talk about someone I love, I look happy, but when Pastor Petrus talked about his god he looked sour as a gherkin." "You are a godless child," said Fröken de Bar, and her nose twitched again because she was angry. "That isn't true at all," I said. "Everything has a god. A blade of grass has an extra-large blade of grass for god and a strawberry has a huge red strawberry for god." Fröken de Bar didn't even answer me, she was so angry. I said, "Fancy, church

being like that! I certainly don't mind terribly that
we can't go again. I wonder why they all stared at us.
Was it because Anna is so beautiful?" Fröken de Bar
simply spluttered. She said, "Ask your Aunt Ninna
why they all stared at you. She'd be able to tell you.
Ask her why she keeps to her room, pretending to
be ill, and doesn't dare show herself in the village.
No wonder Pastor Petrus made an example of her
in his sermon today!" I began to collect spit under
my tongue, but by the time I had got enough together she was far ahead of us. She could hop along
quickly enough, now that she was furious. So I made
a fine snowball with a stone in it instead, and I
aimed it at her and it just knocked that silly green
pompon right off her hat.

22

Anna's Story

Yesterday we did Latin and French in the morning, and in the afternoon we were supposed to do geography, but something exciting happened instead. When I came into our classroom, Jezza and Fröken de Bar were squabbling again. I don't know how it started, but Fröken de Bar was saying, "No, my young lady, no one in his right mind ever travels to places like Zanzibar or Trebizond. If a lady wants to travel she picks out Montreux or Mentone. Those are refined places." "But they don't sound like anything," Jezza said. "What do you mean 'sound'?" asked Fröken de Bar. "Just that, sound," said Jezza. "I want to go to places that sound secret, like Tientsin or Medina or Kabul. Places where one can see and hear and smell things." "Stop it!" shouted Fröken de Bar. "You have crammed your head with a lot of foreign names, but you don't know the first thing about ordinary geography. Why, you can't yet tell me half of the provincial capitals in your own country! And the way you talk about seeing and smelling things! Ugh! When a lady travels she wants to take great care *not* to see anything. First she chooses a good hotel that friends have stayed in time and again and can thoroughly recommend, and of course she never under any circumstances talks to anyone. As to seeing sights, she asks the gentleman at the desk, who in a quiet, respectable hotel is often a man of refinement, to choose a reliable driver to take her about, keeping closely to the fashionable streets where one needn't see the local inhabitants at too close quarters and is sure to find a great many tourists, like oneself." "When does the fun begin?" asked Jezza. Fröken de Bar said, "I don't know what you mean. If one wants a little change one can usually get the hotel to recommend some reliable shop run by respectable ladies, where one can spend a pleasant hour choosing a bit of lace or embroidery. In the evening one of the more cultured guests will frequently play on the piano in the hotel drawing room. Then after one has been there for some time, there may be no harm in exchanging a word or two with the lady at the next table, naturally never asking a question or giving any information about oneself." "Why say anything at all then?" Jezza asked. Fröken de Bar began to get furious and said, "You don't understand anything! It's just like talking to a savage, or to an Eskimo. What a bringing-up you've had!" Jezza said, "When I travel I shall talk to everyone and keep asking questions all day long. I'll run alone about the streets without any silly driver to show me, and I'll stare at all the strange shops with the queer different things in them, and at the exciting men and the lovely ladies. I'll run into houses that look most thrilling and pretend that I've made a mistake. Then they'll ask me to stay, and I'll see everything wonderful they have to show and hear everything funny or sad they have to say, and we'll laugh together and they'll love me, and I'll love them. And when I know everything, I'll travel to the next exciting spot on the map and begin all over again, and in the end I'll know more than any person before. I'll know everything about everything!" "Be quiet!" shouted Fröken de Bar. "You'll do nothing of the kind. Traveling is for distinguished ladies, not for hooligans like you, with your Zanzibars and Kabuls. Besides, you won't have any money and probably you'll stay right here in Berg." Well, Fröken de Bar shouldn't have said that, about Jezza's never being able to travel. Jezza loves names of places, and those places have become her darlings. She shouldn't have told Jezza that she could never see them. I knew it at the time, and I was right. Jezza jumped up. She shouted, "How did you travel at all then, even to your silly Montreux? Frida says that you're only a servant whom we pay, like her. You're no better, you're only a servant." Fröken de Bar stopped being red and got

all white. Her nose twitched. It looked as if it were
made out of rubber. She said in a low voice, a whisper really, "Out you go! Out! Out! Out!" she
whispered to Jezza, looking awfully queer. Then
she did something terrible. Jezza is a big girl, but
Fröken de Bar picked her right up and carried her
out of the room. Jezza's legs are so long that they
hung right down to the floor, and one of them went
out and gave Fröken de Bar's shin a terrible kick.
My, it must have hurt! Fröken de Bar yelled, even
though she is such an aristocratic lady, and she let
go of Jezza. The hall door was open, and we saw
Grandmother walking toward us. Fröken de Bar
tried to run to her but Jezza and I got there first.
Then Fröken de Bar said in the same whispery
voice, "I am leaving, Fru von Stark. I tender my
resignation. I have stood all I could from this dreadful child. I can bear no more." Then someone else
came walking down the hall, and it was Uncle Rolf.
When he came up to us, he took one look at Fröken
de Bar, and fancy what he did. He began to roar
with laughter! When Uncle Rolf needs to laugh
he has to do it right away, he can't stop himself. No
one laughs like Uncle Rolf. He closes his eyes and
opens his mouth so wide that one can see all of his
white, white teeth, and then he really howls. When
Uncle Rolf laughs, the whole house is soon laughing
too, even if nobody knows why. Fröken de Bar did
look funny. Her hair hung down over one ear and
her lace ruffle had got torn and the blouse hung out

of her skirt. I never knew before that she could get untidy. I began to laugh and I heard Frida in the kitchen begin to laugh, and somebody in the sitting room laughed too. From down the hall came the sounds of a polka being played on Aunt Helga's piano, and it sounded just as if the piano were laughing along. Fröken de Bar turned and stalked away, and Uncle Rolf tried to look serious, but he couldn't. He burst out laughing again. "That's Jezza's work," he said. "I recognize it. Oh Jezza, you limb of Satan! The Lord preserve the man who gets you for a wife!" He kept on laughing and he reached into his pocket and gave Jezza a ten-öre piece.

23

Jezza's Story

There is a hole in Auntie Ninna's lung. Doctor Borger says it must have been there a long time, or anyway that there's a spot that's been getting worn, sort of like a stocking when the heel gets thin before the real hole comes. He couldn't bear to tell us after he had examined her, because he loves her so. He went home and wrote a note to Grandmother, telling her, and he sent his housekeeper, Fru Sten, with it. But then a few moments later he came running himself, breathing terribly because he is so fat, and he was carrying on his arm the beautiful red fox rug with the tails of all the foxes that he has shot. He ran upstairs and put it over Auntie Ninna's bed. She must be kept warm, warm, very warm, he said, and looked furiously at all of us. He said that her chest has always been weak and she might have caught a chill that night we ran to his house to play the

gramophone and dance. He told us all her worrying
and being sad and being cooped up in her room had
brought it on with a rush, for people with her illness
never ought to worry. My, but he was angry! He
said he was going to take complete charge of her
from then on, and that nobody should go and worry
her. The white cow, the one who has four good paps
and whom I love, was to be kept in a special stall
and be given oats, just like a horse, to make her milk
more rich. Auntie Ninna would have to drink pints
and pints of it to try to mend the hole. Then Doctor
Borger went away, still furious because he is so terribly in love with her. That was about a week ago.
Today the doctor came into our room after his morning visit to Auntie Ninna, and he said to me, "Listen,
Jezza, go in and try to amuse your Auntie Ninna
from time to time. She likes you better than anyone,
and it's good for her to have you around. Sing something, or tell her stories, but don't get her upset.
Help me to make our Ninna well, little Jezza. Help
me!" I ran to Auntie Ninna's room right away. She
was lying still in her bed doing nothing, not even
playing with the fox tails on the rug, as she used to
do on other days. I said, "You'll soon be well now,
Auntie Ninna darling!" Auntie Ninna looked at me
with her big, big eyes and said, "Who's been teach-
ing you to lie? I thought you and Anna didn't know
how to yet, but I suppose that they've got hold of
you." I didn't answer anything. "You know I'll
never be well again," said Auntie Ninna. "I'll never

be pretty and able to wear my pretty clothes." I said, "Then can I have your hat with the whole black bird on it, Auntie Ninna? I'd love to wear it when I grow up." Auntie Ninna began to cry. She put her face beneath the pillow and cried and cried. I tried to kiss her. I kissed everything there was to kiss, her hair and her shoulders, and then I kissed the rest of her beneath the blankets. I kissed right down her body, and when I came to her feet I bit them a little through the covers like Anna and I do to each other for fun. It was lovely, because she began to laugh then, and she sat up in bed. "I love you through and through, Jezza," she said. "You're the child of my heart. What is going to happen to you out in life I don't know." I said, "I suppose I'll get full of worries pretty soon." "Why do you say that?" asked Auntie Ninna. "Because all grown people are," I said. "They are always worried or sad or angry, and Anna and I don't look forward much to growing up because we'd hate to be sad nearly all the time. I suppose one has to be." Auntie Ninna said, "Yes, one has to be. Sad and wretched and hurt. And wicked too!" She was sitting up straight in bed, and I hoped that the hole wasn't getting any worse. "But you mustn't ever be like that, Jezza," she said. "Never, never! Do you hear me?" She looked so serious, not at all gay, as she usually looks. I said, "How do you mean, Auntie Ninna?" She said, "I mean that you mustn't ever walk over people, the way they have walked over me. And you mustn't let them walk

over you either. You must get away from here and
lead a *big* life. Let the storms toss you about. Oh,
Jezza, I've lived my whole life in a muddle, and
now I'm going to die in a muddle too. I know nothing, nothing." I said, "Anna and I have always
thought that one knew everything when one grew
up. It's all muddly for us now, but that's because
everyone tells us what to feel and what to think,
which isn't at all what we really feel and think."
She said, "It will be the same later on, just the same.
All your life people will try to confuse you and get
you as muddled and stupid and as cruel and narrow
as they are themselves. In the end you become just
like a beetle running up and down in a ditch that's
full of weeds, chasing up one blade of grass, then
down again, darting to the left, darting to the right,
till at last one day someone puts his big heel on you
and crushes you flat. That's what happens in most
people's lives, but it mustn't in yours, Jezza! When
your mama and papa died when you were a little
girl, I decided to watch over you and to see that you
never became stupid and humdrum like other people.
But if I die, I don't know who'll watch over you
then. You have a difficult temperament, you're not
like Anna. But you must promise me, never let your-
self become like the others! Promise me, Jezza."
"Yes, I promise," I said, though I didn't know
awfully well what I was promising. But I think that
way down I did know anyway. I asked her, "Auntie
Ninna, why didn't you ever get away, why didn't

you?" "Yes, why didn't I?" she answered. "I suppose I'm like the cricket, who sings and dances without ever thinking of tomorrow. It's awfully cozy and
comfortable here, even if there never is any ready
cash. There's so much food that it sticks in your
throat, and good things to drink, and fires. In the
back of my mind I always had the thought that I
would get away some day. I dreaded to become like
my sisters, all stodgy and smug. They were always
after me to marry and settle down and become just
like them, but they haven't got me yet, have they?
That's something, even if I didn't get away! It's not
much, but it's something." I said, "I suppose you
didn't have any money for the railroad fare? You
could have asked Uncle Rolf. He always has a
little, and he'd have a lot more if it wasn't for his
tramps. He's awfully generous." "That he is,"
Auntie Ninna said. "But he is the one person I never
could have asked." "Why, Auntie Ninna?" I said,
but she didn't answer for a moment. I thought she
hadn't heard, but then she said, "Because it wasn't
money that I wanted from him, Jezza." She was
silent again and closed her eyes. She kept them closed
for a long time and even when she spoke she didn't
open them. "It's not money that people want from
Rolf," she said at last. "The tramps don't come to
him for money, and it's not his money that that poor
old fool de Bar is after. It's something else, Jezza,
it's something else." She began to cough again, really
terribly this time. She threw herself down and

coughed and coughed, which is just what she shouldn't do, and she was weeping too, though I don't know if that came from the coughing or from what. I remember Doctor Borger's telling me I ought to cheer her up and sing and tell stories, so I said, "Should I ask you some funny riddles, Auntie Ninna? See if you can answer them. Do you know this one? What is it that goes and goes but never gets to the door?" She looked up at me, with her blue eyes all big and dark, and said, "Perhaps I'll ask you a funny riddle too. Why is it that I, who am young and pretty with lots of love inside me, must die, while others who are old and angry can live on? That's the funniest riddle of all, isn't it? It's terribly funny!" She sobbed and sobbed, and her handkerchief was bloody all over, and there was a little blood on the sheet too. I wanted to sing something gay, but there was only cry inside me. I couldn't even tell her that it was the clock that goes and goes but never gets to the door, which is the answer to that riddle and it's the funniest riddle I know. I got into bed with her and we lay and cried.

24

Anna's Story

When the Italian who peddles those plaster statu-
ettes of Jesus and of Venus came around last week,
he said he had to see Grandmother in person, as he
had a letter for her. Frida told him that he lied and
that all foreigners lie, for they're made that way.
He has such sad long mustaches and big wet eyes,
just like Fru Boberg's dog, who got run over last
month. Frida said, "Take off your shoes and I'll let
you go as far as the hall. There's nothing that you
can steal there." He got out of his clogs, and his
feet were wrapped around with straw. He left bits of
straw all over the hall and Frida was furious and
ran after him, picking up the bits as they fell off.
Well, the letter was from Fröken de Bar. It's more
than four weeks since she had that quarrel with
Jezza and left us in a huff, and this was the first time
we'd heard from her. The Italian had sold some

Venuses in Hamar, where Fröken de Bar is visiting her father, and she had given him the letter for Grandmother, as she was afraid to send it by post, since she knows that Frida opens all our letters before we get them and burns the ones she doesn't like. She wrote that she was dying to get back to her little pupils and she never should have taken Jezza's childish prattle so seriously. Her father, the old colonel, was lying sick in the county hospital. She was alone in the world. "Well, what do you think? Should we take her back?" the aunts said to Grandmother. I squeezed Grandmother's fingers to make her say no. We'd been happy without Fröken de Bar these last few weeks, and we'd been lucky, because they hadn't been able to get hold of another teacher. Berg is so terribly far away in the wilderness that no one wants to come here. Grandmother said, "All my life I've never given advice, and I'm over seventy. It would be foolish for me to begin now." The aunts said, "You're no help! You never say anything." "What would you like me to say? That you should take her back or that you shouldn't take her back?" Grandmother asked. "Of course we should take her back!" the aunts answered. Grandmother smiled. "There you are," she said. "You've given the answer yourselves." By dinnertime next day Fröken de Bar was already back. She looked different somehow, not quite so much like a queen. When she kissed us she smelled of something strong. I couldn't think what it was, but Jezza whispered to me, "She smells just like the fiddlers on Midsummer Night. Schnapps." Jezza was right. I recognized the smell as soon as she'd said that. Fröken de Bar's nose was redder than ever. She was dressed in her queenly black dress, and her hair was frizzed and she was pinned together with that brooch with her family's crest cut out in red stone. It is a terribly beautiful brooch, and the little crown above the crest is made of real diamonds. Fröken de Bar could get a lot of money if she sold it, but she'd hang herself first. She says it's been in her family for three hundred years. With the brooch and that dress she would have looked elegant, except for her long red nose. The nose spoiled it all. She said to Grandmother, "I only just now got the news about Fröken Ninna's illness. Karlson told me. How dreadful! A whole lung gone. And to think that a few weeks ago she was dancing her feet off!" Jezza looked furious, as she always does when anyone talks about Auntie Ninna's lung and she glared at Fröken de Bar, who got nervous and walked a few steps away. She must have remembered the awful kick she got that day, and perhaps her shin isn't quite healed yet. When she was standing safely beside Grandmother, Fröken de Bar said, "It was a shock for me to get the news like that, Fru von Stark. A terrible shock! In fact, you know, I feel quite faint." Grandmother said, "Perhaps you'd like a little glass of something, some schnapps or brandy?" "Well, perhaps," said Fröken de Bar, looking happy. "A glass of brandy helps when one's sad." "Anna," said Grandmother, "fetch Uncle Rolf's decanter from the sideboard in the dining room. Would you like a biscuit too?" she asked Fröken de Bar. "Oh, no, no," said Fröken de Bar. "I wouldn't trouble you. Just a little brandy if you'd be so kind." She looked awfully queer, almost crazy, and her nose twitched. I ran off to fetch the decanter, and Jezza came along and said to me, "Do you know what? She isn't a bit sad about Auntie Ninna. She makes her face look mushy but she is all dry inside. I was looking at her and I know it's true." Jezza keeps staring at people's faces the whole time they talk; she doesn't look away a second. She says when they don't mean what they say, they do things with their noses or mouths or eyes. Our aunts all say it's terrible the way Jezza stares at people, never taking her eyes off them for a second, but I suppose she must stare if she wants to find out things. Well, Jezza's nearly always right, but I wonder if she is this time, I mean about Fröken de Bar not being sad. Froken de Bar smells schnapps all day long, and it's simply terrible when she kisses us good-morning and good-night. Perhaps she really is sad, because she said herself that drinking helped one when one was sad, so that may be why she drinks. After breakfast this morning Uncle Rolf went to the sideboard and said, "My word! There's hardly anything left of my brandy. That's queer. I only filled the decanter the day before yesterday." Jezza whispered to me, "Brandy! That's what she smells. It's not schnapps after all, it's brandy." "What's that?" asked Uncle Rolf. "Nothing," Jezza said. "What did Jezza mean?" Uncle Rolf asked me. "I'd be willing to bet she knows who polished off my bottle of brandy." "Anna!" said Jezza, looking hard at me. "Oh, don't worry about her, Jezza," Uncle Rolf said, laughing. "She won't tell. Not Anna of the silent mouth." Uncle Rolf walked off and we had a look at the empty bottle. It was awfully empty. "I wonder if it's a terrible thing to be a drunkard," I said to Jezza, and she answered, "Perhaps it isn't so very terrible. Some have to be drunkards, some don't. That's how it is."

25
Jezza's Story

Auntie Ninna called to me through the wall, "Jezza! Come! Come quick!" I ran in to her room and she was sitting straight up in bed, holding the thermometer in her hand. "Look!" she called out. "Am I seeing wrong? Or is it true that it's right down to normal? Look, Jezza! Look!" I looked at the thermometer and it was true, it was normal. That was the first time I'd seen her sitting up for weeks, and it was lovely. She said, "That makes the third time that I've taken my temperature this morning, but maybe I don't keep it in long enough. Wait, I'll do it once more and keep it in five minutes this time. Then we'll see." She was trembling so that she couldn't keep the thermometer still between her lovely white teeth, and I had to steady it with my hand. All day long Auntie Ninna keeps taking her temperature. She doesn't even care to read or talk any more, but only wants to take her temperature. It's bad for her to keep getting excited, but if Doctor Borger takes the thermometer away, she lies and weeps and says he's trying to hide things from her, so then he has to give it back. He can never say no to her in anything, he loves her so crazily. When the watch said five minutes, I took out the thermometer, but Auntie Ninna snatched it from me and held it close to her eyes. It was normal. We squeezed each other terribly. Then Auntie Ninna said, "You don't think it's stuck, do you? Thermometers often get broken and one doesn't know it. I tell you what, Jezza, you get the thermometer out of Aunt Emilia's room and we'll take my temperature with that one too. We can put it in Eau de Cologne afterwards to kill the germs." So I fetched Aunt Emilia's thermometer, and we held it in Auntie Ninna's mouth another five minutes, and she lay still, looking at me with the thermometer in her mouth and her eyes all shining and looking like stars would look if stars could have long eyelashes all around them. When we took it out, that one showed normal too. Auntie Ninna shouted, "I am going to live! Do you hear! I am going to live, live!" And she said to me, "Darling, run quickly to Doctor Borger's and tell him to come right over. I've got to let him know. He's been working on me so hard and gets happy if my fever goes down half a degree, and now it's gone right down to normal." I ran downstairs so fast that I almost fell, and rushed down the driveway laughing the whole way because I was so awfully happy and there wasn't anyone to see me. The doctor's huge dog came running toward me, and I hugged his head and kissed him. He was so astonished that he forgot to bark. I kicked the door and Fru Sten came hurrying to open it. "Dear me! You frightened me," she said. "What on earth is the matter?" "It's right down to normal, I shouted at her. "Where's the doctor? He must come this minute. Where is he?" She said, " He was to stop at Pastor Petrus' on his way home. The poor pastor's always so constipated, and the doctor has to give him powders over and over again. They taste nasty and his daughters can't get him to swallow them." I said good-bye and ran toward the pastor's farm with Doctor Borger's huge dog galloping alongside of me. The drive leading to Pastor Petrus' house hadn't been cleared since the last snowfall, and I sank in right up to my waist. I wished I had put on my skis. Then the doctor's dog began to bark, and he rushed off to meet his master's sleigh, which was coming down the drive. They almost drove over me before the doctor saw me. I shouted, "It's right down to normal, Doctor Borger!" He picked me up out of the snow and made me say it again and again. "Oh Lord! Lord!" he kept repeating. And he said to me, "Do you know I love your Aunt Ninna more than my work or my health or my money or my life?" Soon he began to act ordinary again and he asked, "Was it she who sent you?" When I said yes, he got all red and shiny, he was so happy she had thought of him before anyone. "What do you say to a little celebration?" he asked. "A little picnic, just the three of us?" "Oh, that's just what Auntie Ninna loves," I said. "She'll make herself pretty and we'll laugh and laugh." We drove back to the doctor's and Fru Sten opened the door. Doctor Borger said to her, "Behold a happy man, Fru Sten, a man who thinks this world a glorious place to live in. Have we anything extra fine and delicious in the larder, Fru Sten? I'm going on a picnic with my love." We went into the kitchen and Fru Sten packed a whole napkinful of the finest things she could find. She tied the four corners and handed it to me. The doctor came crawling up the cellar steps on all fours with spiderwebs in his hair and two beautifully shaped big bottles in his pockets. Fru Sten only had to look at their necks to recognize them. "Why, those are the Château Yqems that we've been saving for years for some special occasion!" she said. "Well, if only the dear lovely lady gets well, this is the greatest occasion we could wish for!" We jumped into the sleigh and Doctor Borger whipped up his horse. If that old horse could have run, I'm sure he would have, he looks so kind. He isn't able to, though. He's like the doctor, too fat. Still, Doctor Borger did run up the whole flight of stairs, right to Auntie Ninna's room. She was sitting up, just as when I left her, straight up, staring at the door with her big, big eyes. Her lovely light curls fell down her back, and she looked just like a little girl. "Lie down, Ninna!" Doctor

Borger shouted. "Lie down and keep warm." He pulled the fox rug right up to her chin. Then he took the thermometer from the table and put it in her mouth and stood holding her wrist. Auntie Ninna lay still with her eyes dark and wide open. "Correct," the doctor said. "Not a scrap of fever." He stood looking down at Auntie Ninna, and she looked back at him. When they had done that a long time, I asked, "When does the fun begin? Can't we begin doing it now?" "Doing what now?" asked Auntie Ninna, her voice all excited, and Doctor Borger said, "Ah, you didn't know that you were invited to a picnic, did you, little Ninna?" He pulled the two lovely bottles out of his overcoat pockets and laid them on the bed, and I began to take the things out of the napkin. "Liver paste with truffles, asparagus tips, jellied goose, lobster tails," I called out. Auntie Ninna said, "Darlings! Oh, you darlings! And with me looking so awful! Jezza, help me make myself a little pretty." I knew that was the first thing she'd think of. I got out her pink swansdown dressing gown and a sky-blue ribbon for her hair and I put her rings on her fingers. They've gotten much too thin, though, for the rings during the weeks she's been lying there in bed. The doctor said, "Supper's served, Madame!" He had laid the table while I had helped her make herself pretty, and it looked terribly elegant. Instead of a flower vase, he'd put in the center a hat of Auntie Ninna's that's all made of flowers. Oh, we laughed! Auntie Ninna said, "I could eat every scrap of food, and drink up all your wine. I'm sick to death of milk. Oh life, wonderful life!" "Steady, steady, little Ninna," said the doctor. "No, no, not steady," cried Auntie Ninna. "Never steady! Drink with me! Let's drink to life, wonderful life!" "To life!" said the doctor, and he got up and stood by Auntie Ninna's pillows. "And now drink to our marriage," said Doctor Borger. "I'll coax you back to real health with my love, and then I'll shut out all unhappiness forever. Please, Ninna. Please!" "Yes, Auntie Ninna," I said. "Please say yes. He wants it so awfully. He'll see that you never get another hole, and we can have lots of picnics and fun. He doesn't look so fat when he stands up either." Auntie Ninna laughed. "All right then, Jezza," she said. "I'll take him. I can't bear to make anyone sad today." The doctor put his face in Auntie Ninna's lap in the fox rug, and he began to cry so that he shook all over. He said, "I've waited so terribly, terribly long. Don't mind me. I'll be all right in a second." Auntie Ninna put her hand in his hair. All her rings had turned outside in, so that the stones didn't show. The fingers were thin and white as twigs when one peels them to make a whistle. She said, "Dear faithful dog! Dear old Harald!" I kissed her other hand and put it inside the neck of my frock and squeezed it there. She looked straight at me, and her eyes were dark and said so many things. She sighed and said, "Oh, Jezza, Jezza! You see, they've caught me after all. They've got me at last, and now I'll never, never get away again."

26

Anna's Story

The ice is splitting. All through the lake it is crumbling up, and last night I dreamed that it was a night in summer and there was a great thunderstorm. When I woke up, a roaring sound was in my ears and the windows were shaking. I still thought that it was thunder, but then I felt my face, and my nose was cold and the hair on my head was cold, so I knew it was winter and the sound I'd heard was that of the ice blocks breaking up. I ran to Jezza's bed and touched her. Her face was cold and unfriendly, just as if Jezza wasn't behind it at all. There came a new roar so loud that all Berg shook, but Jezza slept right on. I thought, now the ice is splitting everywhere, and Uncle Rolf will hear it downstairs in his bed and dream he's about to leave us because spring is coming and the steamboats can get through again. I thought, in every room in Berg there are people ly-

ing in bed with cold empty faces like Jezza's, and all
of them are dreaming of other places, so they're really not in their bodies at all. I got scared, for I was
awake and knew that I was here, but all the others
really weren't here at all. Uncle Rolf was on a boat
going south, and Auntie Ninna was dancing somewhere on a fine ballrom floor, and Grandmother perhaps was walking with dead Grandfather down a
road in Heaven. I ran back to my own bed and I got
my head beneath the sheets and breathed out until it
got a little friendlier down there. I lay like that for
a long time, trying to make it cozy for myself, and
when I looked out again it was almost light. I
thought, now they'll all be coming back to their bodies
from the places where they've been. If I dared to
look out of the window, I'd see them come running
over the snow, blue and chill and light as ghosts, and
those who've been far away running terribly fast for
fear that Frida will get to their rooms with their coffee before they've crept back into their bodies. And
all the time that I was thinking, the ice kept splitting
out there. I could just see the great blocks of ice crack-
ing wide open and breaking apart right down to the
bottom of the lake. The roar was frightful, and I
felt lonely. Ever since Christmas, when Jezza and I
learned that we couldn't feel safe about things, I've
felt sort of lonely and everything has seemed so con-
fused, just like this dark roaring night. When things
happened before, I minded them just when they
happened, and then I forgot them afterwards. Now

I think and think of them, and the more I think, the
less I understand. For instance, there's the thing that
happened yesterday. We'd been to Karlson's to look
at the new pair of twins who are so shriveled and red
they look like old canned tomatoes, and even Fru
Karlson can scarcely look at them, though they are
hers. As we came walking back to Berg, we could see
that Grandmother's four bedroom windows were
flung wide open. She always opens them when she is
very sad or terribly upset. We went indoors just in
time to see Fröken de Bar come out of Grandmother's room, and through the open door we caught a
glimpse of Grandmother sitting by her open window
with her hand before her eyes. We ran into the room,
and Grandmother took her hand from her eyes and
smiled. I nudged Jezza so that she shouldn't ask
Grandmother what was the matter, and she knew
what I meant, all right, but as usual she had to ask
anyway. "What's happened, Grandmother?" she
said. "Something that needn't have happened," answered Grandmother. "Just as there's never any need
for stupid and cruel things to happen." She was standing close by the window, so as to breathe in the fresh
air, and she was staring straight up into the waving
treetops. She looked so sad. On Grandmother's dressing table were standing five empty bottles called
"Martel." They were the same kind of bottles that
we'd seen in Fröken de Bar's wardrobe when we went
to fetch her shawl one night. Jezza said, "Grandmother darling, are you sad because Fröken de Bar

is a drunkard?" "What are you saying, Jezza?" said
Grandmother quickly. "Who has dared call her that
cruel name?" "Nobody," said Jezza. "She just smells
like a drunkard." The door flew open, and Frida
came running in. "Fru von Stark! Fru von Stark!"
she shouted. "Are you going to sack that awful
woman, I'd like to know? Have we had enough of
her, or not? If I hadn't come across those five bottles
in her clothes closet it's I who'd have been blamed for
taking them. She'll soon be as far gone as her father,
the colonel, and he's shut up in an alcoholic asylum,
even though she does call it a nursing home. Are you
going to throw her out, now that she's begun to break
open your sideboards and pick your locks? Are you,
Fru von Stark?" Oh, Frida was in a fury! Grandmother went up to her very close and put her hands
on Frida's shoulders. She said, "I have never thrown
you out, Frida, though my daughters have wanted me
to often because of your bad tempers and your opening of their letters. And why haven't I? Because I love
you. And I love Fröken de Bar. Berg isn't the sort of
house that people are thrown out of, it's a house where
everyone is invited in. Do you know whose fault it is
that Fröken de Bar drinks? Why, it's my fault. Yes,
mine and yours. It's the fault of all of us who haven't
loved her enough. You know, the reason for every
single vice or sorrow is too little love. We give too
little love, Frida. That's the trouble." She put out
her hand to stroke Frida's cheek and said, "So now,
Frida, as we have this big guilt, you and I, I want

(*135*)

you to help me make Fröken de Bar's life bearable.
She has a heavy burden to carry, that craving of hers
for drink. Will you help me, dear old friend?" Frida
threw her apron over her head and wept. She just
shrieked in there. Then she came out of her apron
and she kissed Grandmother's hands and Grandmother's shoulder, and she said, "I will! Yes, I will, dear
Fru von Stark. I'm nothing but an old pile of bones,
but I'd give my life for you. You can have it any-
time, I love you so." She ran out, and we could hear
her sobbing all the way down the stairs. Grandmother said, "I'm tired, my girls. I'm going to sit here
alone a little while, if you don't mind, and look out
my window." Jezza said, "Yes, Grandmother. Only
tell me, can you really love Fröken de Bar? I mean
really love her?" "Yes, Jezza," said Grandmother,
"I can really love her. You see, some people give us
one chance, or many chances, every day to love them.
They are wonderful people. They are people like
your Uncle Rolf. But everyone, no matter how un-
pleasant, will sometime, if only for the flash of a
second, make it possible for us to begin to love him.
Watch for that moment! Watch for it, my Jezza,
with your quick eye, for I tell you that it is worth
waiting for." Jezza said, "Yes, Grandmother, I will
watch. You always tell us to do things differently
from the way other people want us to do them. I
think you must be different from everybody else in
the whole world, Grandmother!" Grandmother answered, "If I am different, child, it is because I've

taught myself to be different by looking at life with wide-open eyes. I've tried hard to rescue my soul from people's destructions, my darling from the lions, as it says in the psalms. And I've done so by thinking my own way and by acting my own way. Do the same, little Jezza, for your 'darling' is terribly worth saving."

27

Jezza's Story

I asked everyone in the house how soon the anemones come after the first snowdrops. Nobody seemed to know. Karlson was the only one who had an inkling. He said one can find them about ten days later on sunny slopes, but that they were especially late this year. He said he hadn't seen one yet, and I don't wonder at that, because I've looked all about and I haven't seen one either. Then he asked me why I wanted to know, and I told him it was because Auntie Ninna was pining for anemones. Every time I come into her room after I've been out, she looks at my hands, and when she sees that they're empty, she sighs and says that spring is never coming this year. That's why I said to Anna yesterday that we must go out looking for anemones. If anyone could find them it would be Anna, for she knows the forest as if she were one of the foxes that live in it, and she just sniffs out where to go for flowers or for mushrooms or for anything. Well, we went in the afternoon, and we hunted for hours and hours, but there wasn't a single anemone out, not one. I said, "When we come home, I'll have to sit in our room a while to get rid of the smell of forest before I go in to see Auntie Ninna. If she knew that I'd been out today and hadn't found a single flower she'd burst out weeping. She is feeling so sad, now that her fever has begun to climb again." I had just finished saying that, and I was looking at Anna's face, guessing what she would answer, when I heard a noise. Right behind us there were steps, terribly heavy steps, just like a herd of elk coming. I was so scared I gave out a yell, but there wasn't anything to be scared about. It was people that I'd heard, and suddenly they were standing right beside us. It was the four Petrus ladies, the daughters of the pastor. They were scared too, coming on us so deep in the forest, where nobody ever goes. They stood still and stared at us. It was dark where they were standing, and where we were standing it was dark too, but right between us there was a clearing, hot and sunny, and we all ran out to it and began laughing and saying how-do-you-do. It was really lucky, because we've never been allowed to get acquainted with the Frökens Petrus, and the aunts don't see them either, because of Pastor Petrus being their father and because Pastor Petrus called Grandfather a suicide just because he was a Last Viking. They were tall and enormous, the Frökens Pet-

rus, and so ugly that it just hurt one to look at them.
Their faces were like soup plates and they had white
eyelashes and tiny little eyes, just like the whale in
that picture of the whale hanging in our classroom,
on which it says underneath that one can put sofas
and chairs right inside his head and sit there, but that
his eyes aren't much larger than walnuts. We'd often
seen the Frökens Petrus from far off on the road,
but near to they looked much huger, and they looked
terribly poor somehow. We looked at them, and they
looked at us, and then the biggest one of all said,
"Oh, this must be Anna! Isn't she a darling? Oh, how
beautiful she is!" They all four stared at Anna and
nodded to her and smiled. People always smile when
they look at Anna, just as if they were pleased with
her for being as beautiful and lovely as she is. The
same one said, "Forgive us for staring, but we've always wanted to see Anna. We see so few beautiful
things, and everyone in Berg Village talks about her.
Even in Bo, where we go to play the organ at the
Seamen's Mission, people have asked us if it's true
that she's so beautiful. Oh, and it is true! It is!" "I
hope we didn't scare you?" asked one of the other
sisters. I said, "You did. I thought you were a herd
of elk. We are looking for anemones for our Auntie
Ninna, who is ill." "Oh, we know," they all said at
once, and one of them went on alone, "We have been
so sad about your aunt, although we don't know her.
We ask Doctor Borger about her every time he comes
to see Papa. Isn't she any better?" "Yes, she is," I

said, for I didn't want them to think she was so awfully ill. "We had a picnic a few weeks ago and she
sat up in bed and put on her swansdown dressing
gown. Her rings turned inside out because her fingers had gotten thin. She has fever again now, but as
soon as spring comes I know she'll get well." The
most enormous of the Frökens Petrus said, "Oh yes,
I'm quite sure, too," and she turned to look at the
others, as if she wanted them to say it too. "Yes, yes,
it's quite certain. As soon as spring comes," they all
said at once. They were always saying things at the
same time. "We must trust in the Good Shepherd,"
said one of them. "In whom?" I asked. "Jesus," she
said. I said, "What has He got to do with it? He's
dead. He had terrible pains when He died Himself,
and I'm sorry for Him, but I'm just as sorry for
Auntie Ninna, who gets soaked with sweat every time
she coughs and has to look at her own blood come
trickling out. She says it looks alive and gay and that
she hates to think of her gay red blood running away
from her." "You talk so queerly, dear," said the biggest Fröken Petrus. "Just like a little savage. One
isn't supposed to talk so freely. It isn't nice. Of course
we know that you haven't been brought up in God.
Oh dear, oh dear! Still, I do hope that your aunt
will soon be hale and hearty, I do truly." She looked
so kind when she said it, I knew she was the one who
likes Doctor Borger and whom everyone in Berg Village wants Doctor Borger to marry so that he'll
have someone to come home to after a hard day's

work. It's only the doctor himself who doesn't want it. So it was extra kind of her to wish for Auntie Ninna to get well when she knows that it's lovely Auntie Ninna whom Doctor Borger wants for a wife. There's something I can't understand at all. Pastor Petrus is sniveling and hypocritical, just as Grandfather said most pastors were. I saw that the day we went to church. But though he's like that, his daughters aren't hypocritical at all. The big one really meant it when she said she wanted Auntie Ninna to get well. I mean she *really* meant it. I know people from looking at their faces, and I know that the four Frökens Petrus are nice in every bit of their bodies, in spite of being daughters of a sniveling father. Everything is to terribly muddly nowadays! Then the same one, the one Doctor Borger would rather not marry, said, "Have you looked in the hollow behind High Rock? The flowers are always early there. Oh, we'd love to come along and help you look! May we?" We walked together to High Rock. Twigs and even big branches snapped like matches when the Frökens Petrus stepped on them, their feet were so huge and heavy, and their boots looked like the old boots we sometimes find in ditches and wonder who has thrown them there. They're terribly poor at the pastor's farm. They never have meat, Frida says, and at every meal the pastor doles out ten huge potatoes to each of his huge daughters—that makes forty potatoes, and that's all they get to eat. Well, when we got to High Rock there wasn't a single anemone there either. The

Frökens Petrus saw that we were awfully sad, and they looked at each other as if they were trying to think of where to take us next to find something springlike to take home to Auntie Ninna. Suddenly one of them said, "Listen! Listen!" and looked up into the sky, though there wasn't much sky to be seen because of all the pines. She whispered, "They're coming! They're coming! Don't you hear the wings?" Oh, it was wonderful! A whole flock of wild geese came flying in the sky, the first to come home from Africa, great, great white geese. The Fröken Petrus who wants to marry Doctor Borger grabbed Anna by the hand and began running with her up High Rock, and we all ran after them. We were all laughing. It had been so wonderful to see them coming, white and huge, and not a bit tired after their enormous journey. When we got to the top, we could see the whole sky, and there were the wild geese, just above us! The leader goose made a turn and dropped a little lower, and the others came right behind him. For a moment, they all circled around and around just above the rock, as if they knew we were standing there, loving them. Then they stretched their necks out before them and formed a triangle again and sailed away like lovely ships in the sky, and we stared and stared after them. The huge Fröken Petrus had tears in her eyes. She wiped them with her hand and said, "Oh, how far away they have been! How beautiful they were!" All four of them looked at each other as if they knew just what she meant, that they were so ugly and heavy, and without wings, and had never been far away and would never be going anywhere all their lives. I wanted awfully to say something nice to them, but nothing came. I just said, "We have never been far away either, Anna or I. We've only been to the fair in Bo." They said, two of them at the same time, "Oh yes, to Bo! We have often been to Bo, too. But Hulda has been as far as Hamar with Papa and Gusten, haven't you, Hulda?" They said that to the one who ought to marry Doctor Borger, so I suppose her name is Hulda. She certainly looked like a Hulda— one couldn't have thought of squeezing her or of having her sit cozily on one's lap. Hulda said, "Oh yes, I have been to Hamar! I should say so. It was about twelve years ago, and I'll never forget it. Such chocolates they had at the confectioner's, thirty different kinds! I got one with Kirsch liqueur inside, and how surprised I was! I was scared Papa should get to hear of my drinking intoxicants, but the shop-girl laughed when I told her. She had a velvet bow in her hair. It was nice, that bow, but it wouldn't have suited everyone. Oh, it all seems like yesterday!" "And Hulda went to a ball!" one of the sisters said. "Yes, I did. Can you imagine it?" said Hulda. "I have never confessed it to Papa, though I've wanted to every Sunday for these twelve years. I'm sure it was a wicked thing to do, but it was lovely. Such beautiful clothes everybody had, pink and green, like ice cream! I had the most wonderful time. Oh, I've never had such fun! I danced the whole night through with my brother, Gusten." One of the sisters who hadn't said anything yet—she seemed to have mustaches on her face—said, "It must have been lovely for you, dear! I am happy for your sake, having such a lovely memory to cherish. I'm afraid it was dreadfully wrong, though." "Yes, yes, dreadfully wrong," said the other three quickly. "All worldly gaiety is wrong, very wrong." I said, "No, it's right to be gay. One should be terribly, terribly gay. That's what I think. I am going to be terribly gay and happy always." The Hulda one said, "How do you know, child? Very likely you will have many sorrows, like all of us." I said, "What has that got to do with being happy? I'll be gay all the same." "Now you're talking queerly again, dear," said Hulda. "You frighten me, you really do. I can't think what my papa would say if he heard you." "Oh, that reminds me," said one of the others. "Papa must be waiting for us and getting furious. It's late. He'll be wanting his lamp lit. We must hurry." Suddenly they all looked scared, and we began walking home, so quickly it was almost like running. At the entrance to the village we turned to the left, they turned to the right. Anna and I had gone a little farther when Hulda came running after us. She was all out of breath, and she said, "Please tell your Auntie Ninna about the wild geese. Be sure to do that! She'll know then that spring has come. They're a much surer sign of spring than the anemones, and she can lie and listen for the sound of their wings. Please tell her just how they came flying, and how their wings shone, and how they flew up higher and higher, right into the sky. Will you tell her that, dear? It will help her, I know it will. It has helped me often, often, to think of them." And so we took the wild geese back to Auntie Ninna instead of the anemones.

28

Anna's Story

Uncle Rolf and I think each other wonderful. Something happened before supper, just before the sun went down. He said something lovely, and afterwards, when we came home, we looked at each other over the supper table, and he smiled at me. I smiled right back, which is a thing I've never done with anyone before, excepting Jezza. After supper I told her what had happened when Uncle Rolf and I were looking at the tree. It was something very special, though I suppose there are many people in the world besides Uncle Rolf and me who like to stand looking at a tree when the wind blows crazy, as it did today, and who feel like saying, "More! More! Oh, bravo! Bravo!" as a big branch swings out and down and makes a lovely bow at one. I was standing by the lake looking for shells for Fru Karlson's canary bird to sharpen his beak on, seeing that Fru

Karlson can't go out nowadays to get shells herself. She has to stay home to take care of that red pair of twins who look like canned tomatoes. There was a spring windstorm going on, and the green reeds lay flat on the water, with the black waves washing right over them. Uncle Rolf came wading out of the reeds with his gun and his big wading boots and a red handkerchief tied about his head, for no cap could have stayed on in that howling storm. Mine wouldn't. It blew off and went flying right toward Uncle Rolf and stopped at the edge of the water. I had been wanting to run away, for I hate to be with people when Jezza isn't there to answer them in case they speak to me. Now I had to go and fetch my cap. Uncle Rolf was standing looking at that big birch tree that grows on the shore, and the wind was whistling through its branches as if a gay boy were hiding there, whistling away. The waves in the lake were white with froth, and it was fine to see the water running free again after it had lain cooped up under black ice all winter. That howling wind kept blowing from the lake, and it sounded the way Frida says the bears used to sound when they came roaring down from the mountains when she was young and there were hundreds of bears. It was then that the birch tree was so wonderful. The big branches reared themselves in the air, shook themselves wildly, and bent down again, almost far enough to snap. Then they straightened themselves and threw themselves backwards, and sideways, just as horses do when

they toss their heads, and then they swept down-
wards with a great swish, making their bow. Oh, it
was fine! And as we stood looking, Uncle Rolf said
that lovely thing. He said, "Bravo! Bravo!" and
he clapped his hands, as if we were at a theater. How
wonderful that he should have said what I've often
felt like saying! For instance, when the water hits the
big rock in the lake and it goes "Boom!" or in the
evening when the sun makes Berg red as a red rose
before going down, or in the morning when the grass
is covered with little drops of water that came there
in the night when the grass was silent and lonely as
it likes to be—at all those times I've felt like shouting "Bravo! Oh, bravo!" All at once I loved Uncle
Rolf. I hadn't before, at least not all through me,
but then I did. I kissed his hand. He took it away,
and I thought he was angry, but he looked awfully
glad. "Why did you do that?" he said. "Because of
something you said," I told him, "but I don't want
to tell you what." Uncle Rolf said, "You never need
tell me anything. I will learn to understand without
your speaking. I will learn the Anna-language that
has no words, even though it may take me a whole
lifetime." I thought a while and then I said, "A lifetime means all your life, and won't you have to leave
us now, when spring has come, and go to your own
home, Uncle Rolf?" "Yes—perhaps," he said, and
looked unhappy. "The boats have begun to run
again. In fact, it's strange that I haven't heard from
my family." Well, that wasn't so awfully strange.

I could have told him why he hadn't heard. As soon as a letter in an elegant cream-colored envelope comes nowadays, Frida burns it in the stove. Yesterday she ran around with her apron over her head and shrieked, "I've done it! I've done it again! It's wrong of me, but now it's done!" Then she poked the fire, but the paper that his family uses is so expensive and thick it burned for a long time. She poked it with the iron and kicked it with her big boot and kept saying that his family wasn't ever going to get him back if she had any way of stopping it. But naturally I couldn't say all that to Uncle Rolf. Mouths that tell are as stupid-looking as kitchen sieves, Grandmother says. Anyway, I wouldn't have had time, for just then we caught sight of someone coming toward us, far down the road, and I could tell from his fatness that it was Doctor Borger. He was hanging onto his hat with one hand, carrying his doctor's bag in the other. I said, "It will feel funny to call Doctor Borger 'Uncle Harald.' We'll have to soon, won't we, as he's Auntie Ninna's fiancé?" "I hope so with all my heart," said Uncle Rolf. "But Ninna was dreadfully ill again this morning and she's been lying weeping all afternoon. Poor Ninna! She never would be friends with life, but always wanted it different than it was. And now she doesn't want to be friends with death either." I said, "She isn't going to die, is she? She is going to marry." "That would be the same thing for Ninna," said Uncle Rolf. I said, "If Auntie Ninna only would stop weeping! Even Fröken de Bar, who says such nasty things about her, can't bear to think of her weeping because she wants so badly to live. Yesterday she went into Auntie Ninna's when no one was noticing, and she took off her gold brooch with the crest, which is the only valuable thing she owns, and she pinned it on Auntie Ninna's nightgown. She asked Auntie Ninna to promise her that she would stop crying and get well, so that she could wear the brooch at a ball. She must have known that what Auntie Ninna wants more than anything is to go to one more ball. Auntie Ninna told Jezza about it, and we can't believe that awful Fröken de Bar could be so lovely." Uncle Rolf said, "Don't ever underestimate people, little Anna. Every one of them, yes, every one, has the possibility of greatness." By now Doctor Borger was getting closer, hurrying along the road while we stood on the beach. He'd been running, and he's so terribly fat that he was all out of breath. He was red in the face, too. He looked frightened. "What's happened, Borger? What's happened?" shouted Uncle Rolf, making a funnel of his hands so that he could be heard through the storm. Doctor Borger shouted back, "Ninna's just had a hemorrhage. I'm on my way to her now."

29
Jezza's Story

We were doing lessons in the classroom when Uncle Rolf came galloping up to the window and shouted, "Look what I have in my hat!" We ran to the window. His black mare was dancing on her hind legs and she was all shiny with sweat. Uncle Rolf laughed and pushed his hat back on his head, and then we saw what he had stuck in the ribbon. It was a blue anemone! We laughed and sniffed at the air, and it certainly did smell like spring. "Where did you find it, Uncle Rolf?" asked Anna. He said, "Would you really like to know?" Then he stretched up his arms and lifted Anna right out of the window and put her on his saddle in front of him. They are real friends now, and Anna isn't a bit shy with him any more. Fröken de Bar cried, "But I can't let her off right now in the middle of her lesson!" and Uncle Rolf laughed as if she'd said something idiotic. "It'll

be a much better lesson for her to see the first anemones," he answered. Then they galloped off. He
laughed and waved his hat at us, and soon all we
could see were the mare's hoofs and her long black
tail flying after her through the trees. At lunch
Grandmother said, "It's really time to take out the
double windows. Such wonderful sunshine! It smells
spring today, doesn't it?" Frida said, "It may smell
spring, but it isn't. No, Fru Stark, it isn't the right
date for taking out the double windows, and I am
not going to touch them yet." But after lunch Grandmother began to pull away the cotton wadding between the windows, and so did Anna and I. Frida
ran around wringing her hands. She threw her apron
over her head and said, "I can't stand seeing you do
it. You don't know how, and you are getting everything messed up. Get out, all of you. I'll do it myself, though it breaks my heart." She made us get
out of the sitting room and locked the door. We
laughed. Grandmother said, "It's the same every
year. She can't bear changes. Every change upsets
her, dear old Frida!" A little later we saw Gudrun
and Karna carrying pails across the yard and Karlson
bringing the stepladder. They all climbed in through
the dining-room window, and we could hear Frida
bellowing orders at them. They went about from
one room to another, taking out the winter windows
and washing the other ones. By coffee time every
winter window was out, the cotton wadding was all
gone, and the other panes looked just as clear as

water. Anna and I went around putting our fingers on them, because it seemed that they would go right through, as if there weren't glass there at all! The whole house looked yellow from the sun pouring down on it. Everyone went around sniffing the air and asking each other, "Doesn't it smell like spring today?" Each time the front door opened, we could hear the sound of water running down the hill, gurgling and spitting, the snow was melting away so quickly. We ran in and out of every room, opening windows. We couldn't sit still, everything was so terribly gay. We had our afternoon coffee in the hall, though it was still chilly in there. Frida said that if it was spring she was going to serve the coffee spring-fashion in the hall, whether we liked it or not. She said that she was sick of fighting. If we wanted it to be spring, it could be spring for all she cared. She slammed every door hard, but she wasn't really furious. I knew that because she'd put some of the lovely blue anemones that Uncle Rolf and Anna picked in a vase on the coffee table, and she kept moving the vase each time she came in so as to keep them right in the sun. Most of the anemones were up in Auntie Ninna's room, because we all wanted her to know that lovely gay spring had come. All at once my legs began to feel hoppy, the way they sometimes do—really crazy, they felt. There was music. "What's that?" I asked. I ran to the hall window and opened it wide. Frida said, "It's Sven. He's even more crazy than usual today because of the weather.

(*154*)

He's gone to fetch his fiddle." Oh, how he played! He is such a grand fiddler, Sven. He was wearing his red knitted cap and was sitting on a wheelbarrow full of dung, with sparrows hopping about in it, pecking and making a crazy gay noise. He played even louder than they screeched, then they began screeching louder, and he played louder still. He played and played, and his bow just danced. But then there came another noise, a horrible one this time. It sounded like something splitting. I knew that it was Auntie Ninna coughing, but coughing terribly, terribly, as never before. The sound seemed to be coming closer. We couldn't understand. We all jumped up and looked at the staircase, and there was someone standing right at the top. It was Auntie Ninna! She was in her nightgown and she was white, oh so white! In her hand she had all the anemones, and she held them pressed to her heart. She stood looking at the open window and listening to Sven's fiddle, and then suddenly she began to run. Now she was looking at us, and her eyes were so big, and as blue as the sky outside the window. She hurried right down the stairs and came running toward us. Then she lifted her arms in the air and called out loud, very loud, "I am dying! I am dying!" She fell to the floor, and at once everyone was beside her. She shook her head as if saying "no" to someone, and then she turned it to one side. Her lips became red, red. It was her blood. The blue anemones had fallen to the floor and her hand lay open upon them.

Her bare feet were right in a patch of sunlight, and I don't think I'd ever really looked at her feet before. I'll always remember them now. Such darlings! So thin and white they were, and just ready to run. Grandmother had her hand on Auntie Ninna's heart. She said, "Oh, oh!" and she put her hand over her own eyes. There was such a noise coming in through the window—the fiddle, and the running hoppy water, and the sparrows twittering, so terribly gay. I looked at Auntie Ninna to see if she was listening. Her long hair was spread out over the floor in a thousand curls. I thought, "She shouldn't lie there on that cold floor. It's bad for her." No one was moving. They were still and they all looked somehow astonished. Then I knew that she was dead and that it didn't matter that she lay on the floor in her thin nightdress. Oh, that was terrible to think of! I screamed, "Anna! Anna!" and I felt Anna's face right close to mine.

30
Anna's Story

A lady came yesterday. She was carrying a bag and she walked upstairs on tiptoe. She was fat and white, and she had come to dress Auntie Ninna. It's queer. One must have a special death dress, just as one has a ball dress or a sport dress. She stayed on and on in there. I suppose it's difficult to dress a dead lady, as she can't help much by sitting up or putting her arms through or anything. Jezza couldn't bear thinking of her fussing about with Auntie Ninna like that. She ran away, out into the garden, but quite soon she came running back, up all the stairs, and asked, "Is she gone?" "No," I said. She ran away again and came back almost at once. "Now is she gone?" she said. "Not yet," I told her. The others are scared about the way Jezza goes on since Auntie Ninna lay down and died. She can't sit still, or eat, or anything, and she has such a terrible ache inside her from being sad. I remember that Grandmother once said, "From the day one takes up one's first big sorrow, one will always carry sorrow. One wears a pack upon one's back, and though what's inside it may change many times during one's life, one can never lay down that pack for a single day. Every morning one has to fling it on one's shoulder." So I'm trying to help Jezza carry her pack. I don't leave her for a moment, I hold onto her hand from morning till night. When the lady had left and we had gone to bed for the night, I knew that Jezza hadn't curled up, as one does when one is ready to sleep. She lay straight and stiff as a stick. I got into bed with her so that we could hold each other, and I twisted my leg around one of hers to make it feel happier. I pulled the bedclothes over our heads and I said, "I love you as much as all the world." She said, "I love you too, but I can't feel it now. I am aching and aching for Auntie Ninna." I asked her, "But you don't ache as much as if I were dead instead?" She said, "I wouldn't ache then, I'd die. Promise me that I won't live if you ever die. Promise me, Anna!" I said, "I will, if you promise that I won't live if you die. I hope that we can keep our promises." Jezza said, "We can if we love enough," and I answered, "I do love enough." We squeezed each other terribly and we couldn't breathe at all down there, it was so hot. We stuck our heads up. The room was black. Jezza said, "I'm scared to think of Auntie Ninna now. I'm sure that she looks horrible, like that dead goat we saw in the ditch. Do you remember? His teeth had fallen right out of his mouth and lay in front of him in the mud, and his legs stuck right out stiff. Do you think Auntie Ninna looks like that yet?" "Yes," I said, "I suppose she does. We'll see her tomorrow. Grandmother said that we'll all go in and see her before the funeral." Jezza asked, "Do you think they'll be awful and sneering to Auntie Ninna, as they were at Christmas? If they are, I'll bite them. I *will* bite them, Anna!" "Yes," I said. Jezza said, "You mustn't leave me now. It's awfully hot, with both of us in one bed, but don't go away. I can't sleep if I am alone and think of Auntie Ninna lying in the next room looking like that goat. I'll never be able to sleep alone any more, I'll always think of her. I'll have to have a terribly thin man to be in bed with when I grow up. You're pretty thin, but it's hot anyway. He'll have to be like a rod." We turned away from each other, because one's back side is never as hot as the front, but each time I began to go to sleep Jezza gave my behind a push with hers so as to keep me awake. At last she didn't push any more, so I knew she was asleep. Today Aunt Emilia and Aunt Helga arrived from town with Uncle Staffan and Uncle Viktor, and Aunt Petronella came too, on the three-o'clock train. When they drove up in the carriage, we couldn't tell which was which. All three of them had black stuff hanging down over their faces. What a lot of dressing-up there's been! First Auntie Ninna getting a new dress

just for being dead, and then our aunts hanging
black stuff over their faces. They kissed Grandmother and us through the stuff, and it felt queer.
Then they walked upstairs, the aunts first, and then
their husbands, in single file. It looked like a game.
Frida had kept weeping and howling so terribly that
she wasn't allowed to come along. Grandmother
opened the door to Auntie Ninna's room, and it was
wonderful in there with all the windows open and
the sun pouring in. The birds sang like crazy and
they flew with twigs in their beaks in the trees outside. Jezza whispered to me, "You look first. If her
teeth are lying outside of her I won't go in." I felt
scared too. I couldn't swallow. I watched all the
other faces first to see how they looked on seeing her,
and they all looked sweet. I looked at the bed quickly
with just one eye, and Jezza must have looked at
the same time, for her hand left mine and she ran by
everyone, right up to the bed. "Look! Look!" she
called. "She isn't dead at all. Isn't she lovely with
the anemones in her hair? Look, she has a bouquet
in her hand, too! She is smiling. She's well again now,
isn't she?" Everyone began to sob terribly. Grandmother said, "Poor little Jezza! Poor passionate
heart! In you Ninna is certainly still alive and always will be." We all kissed Auntie Ninna's hand.
It was cold. We went down into the hall and Karna
served everyone hot wine. She had an elegant frill
around her neck. Jezza ran around and was happy
because Auntie Ninna had been so beautiful and smil-

ing and had worn flowers in her hair and carried a
bouquet, just as if she were going to a lovely ball.
Then something happened, something wonderful.
Fröken de Bar came up to Jezza and said quickly,
not at all the way she usually talks, "I have never
seen anyone so lovely as your Auntie Ninna was today. Never." She walked away quickly, but oh, how
fine it was of her, who was grown up, to apologize
like that to Jezza for having said nasty things about
Auntie Ninna! Jezza got all red, and she looked at
me. Then she ran after Fröken de Bar and caught
her just by the door, and she hugged her terribly
and kissed her all over her face and didn't seem to
mind about the nose. Fröken de Bar began to cry.
She said, "Dear, dear child! Thank you. Thank you.
It's all very difficult. One gets so little love. I don't
know. It's all very difficult."

31
Jezza's Story

Yesterday a letter came for Uncle Rolf from his family. This one Frida didn't steam open because she's been having dizzy spells, and when she met Pastor Petrus on the road the other day he told her that her maker might be gathering her to His bosom, so she must stop sinning in order to meet him as white as the driven snow. Well, Frida's main sin was opening other people's letters, and everyone is sorry that she's stopped, as one used to be able to tell from her face whether it was bad news or good news, and then prepare oneself beforehand. Because of her new sinlessness she had put the letter on Uncle Rolf's breakfast table, beside his piping hot eggs. Then she ran to the pantry, from where she could see what was happening. Frida told us later that she'd expected Uncle Rolf to look furious on hearing from his nagging brother again, but this time he just sat

staring at the letter with no expression in his face
at all. Suddenly he did the queerest thing, Frida
said. He broke open one of his soft-boiled eggs,
scooped out some of the white sticky goo, and stuck
down the flap of the envelope. "Frida! Frida!" he
shouted, and when she came running, Uncle Rolf
told her he'd misplaced his reading glasses, so would
she please read the letter aloud to him. That's why
Frida says now that Uncle Rolf is the kindest person
in the world, because he wanted to give her the joy
of breaking the glad tidings. The news was that his
dropsical brother had dropped dead. As he hadn't
ever liked that scolding mean brother, no one could
feel sorry. And now Uncle Rolf would be coming
into some money. "Then I'll satisfy some of those
secret desires that everyone carries inside them," he
told Frida. "Jezza longs to travel. Now I can buy
her all the tickets she wants. The tramps want more
schnapps. I'll get them a barrelful. And what is *your*
secret desire, Frida?" he asked her. "To stay in Berg
and look after you and Fröken Anna and all the
children you are going to have," Frida answered.
"That's my desire too!" Uncle Rolf said, laughing.
"And mine," said Anna, when Frida told her later
on of that chat with Uncle Rolf. Of course Aunt
Emilia couldn't let on how pleased she was. "I suppose you'll be looking after your own place from now
on," she said gloomily. "We won't be seeing much
of you any more, Rolf." How I hated her! But
Uncle Rolf didn't pay Aunt Emilia any attention

at all. He went up to Grandmother, who was sitting near a vase filled with branches of lilac. He bent his knee and knelt before her. "If I may continue to look after Berg in my fashion, it will be the greatest honor you can confer on me," he told her. Grandmother put her small hands on his broad shoulders and she said, "No one can 'confer' anything on you, Rolf. It's you who confers things on others by—by being Rolf." Uncle Rolf blushed dark. It was because of what he read in Grandmother's eyes.

32

Anna's Story

A lawyer in black stepped out of a carriage and sneezed three times. He said, "Excuse me, I have hay fever. I want to see Mr. Heller about something very important. So I brought him to Uncle Rolf's office, where by good chance there were no tramps, excepting only The Poet. "My business is *very* confidential. Could we be alone?" said the lawyer, looking hard at The Poet's shoes without laces and his coat of rags. "No," answered Uncle Rolf. "No one has secrets from anyone in Berg. It's that kind of house." Uncle Rolf had been sort of grumpy ever since he got that letter from his sister-in-law. He didn't laugh in the same way, and he didn't laugh nearly as often. Now the lawyer sneezed again and asked, "Where is the ink, please?" "There isn't any ink," Uncle Rolf answered. "As I don't believe in keeping accounts, what is the point of having ink?"

So then the lawyer took two ink bottles and two pens from his brief case, one for the red ink and one for the black. He put one pen behind each flapping ear and was ready for business. "I suppose you've come about my inheritance?" Uncle Rolf asked him, sounding not at all happy. The lawyer answered, "Ye-es. Well, in fact, no." He took a lot of papers out of his briefcase, but Uncle Rolf said, "Don't bother about those, please. I hate papers. Just tell me how much money I'm to get." The lawyer sneezed again, and then he said in a sort of heavy voice, "None!" Uncle Rolf burst out laughing. He threw both arms about the lawyer, and he shouted, "What a relief! Oh, *what* a relief! You see, my dear fellow, I was worrying about all that money and what to do with it. And a happy man never worries. Do you know, this is the most wonderful news!" The lawyer looked at Uncle Rolf, frowning, and began to explain how the debts had eaten up all of the estate, seeing that the dropsical brother's wife had bought too many clothes and given far too many dinner parties. As he was going into details, I heard the carriage horses stamping by the front steps and I ran off to say good-bye to Gösta and to Pär. They're being packed off to Hamar to be coached by a tutor in the subjects they're worst in. They are worst in every subject, but they're so terrible in math they can't understand why two and two make four. "Why do they?" they ask everyone. "What *is* four anyway? Why must two twos make a four?" Jezza gave a sugar lump to Thor and another to Ajax, and called good-bye to those two idiots, who were sitting in the carriage, sniveling away. Uncle Rolf came hurrying. He patted Pär's and Gösta's cheeks, which were wet with tears. "Don't fret about two and two making four," he consoled them. "There's something more important than that." "Oh, what?" they sobbed in chorus, and Uncle Rolf whispered something in their ears. They were looking a little happier as Thor and Ajax trotted them off to the tutor in Hamar. "What did you whisper to Gösta and Pär?" Jezza asked Uncle Rolf. "I mean, what is it that's more important than knowledge, which Fröken de Bar tells us is the most important thing in the world?" Uncle Rolf answered, "Happiness! *That's* the most important thing in the world." He looked at me, and I looked right back at him, for I'm not shy with him any more since that day when we stood on the beach and he shouted "Bravo!" to the birch tree. And I'm not worried that he may be going away, for now I know he's decided to stay in Berg and to marry me, and we'll have as many children as I used to have dolls, dozens perhaps.

33

Jezza's Story

It's a long time since I've written in my book, and Anna hasn't written either. It's much harder to sit down and write when the sun's shining and everything's green and new outside. It's real summer weather now, and tomorrow, the first of June, Uncle Rolf's old friend from his university days is coming to stay, as he does every summer, even though he is the busiest man on earth. Natanael Krug is so busy he's always out of breath from dashing around the world looking for new books to bring to our country, which is cooped up so far north on the map. He is a terribly famous publisher, and that is an extra reason for me to love him, for of course publishers are men who print writers' books, and I'm going to be a writer. Natanael himself said that I ought to. "A writer is a person who stares at everything from morning till night and from youth till old age, and you certainly know how to stare, you hooligan," he said to me, and then he laughed. Next to Uncle Rolf, he likes me better than anyone at Berg, and I like him so much that, when he arrives, I run round and round him in circles. But other guests also have arrived to spend the holidays, Gunhild and Pär and Gösta. They certainly are boring. They never change from one year to another, but yesterday there was a little change in Gunhild; her blouse was puffed out in front. In the afternoon when we were all standing naked in the bath house, we saw that it was her breasts that stuck out like that. They didn't do it at Christmas time. I went up to her and touched one of them. Cousin Gunhild jumped away and said, "What are you doing? How awful you are!" I said, "What do you mean? They look nice. Most of you is terrible, but they are really nice. Anna and I will soon be getting ours. They are for milk, you know." I thought I'd better explain to Gunhild, because she never understands anything and is silly, as Frida says all town people are. Gunhild said, "How dare you talk like that? Anna and you are naughty girls; you know all sorts of things that nice girls shouldn't know. I'll tell my mother on you." "You'll tell her what?" I asked her. "Doesn't she know yet? Breasts are the same as udders, only they are stuck on in a different place because we walk on two legs and cows on four." When we swam out onto the lake it was blue and hot. Anna and I were fishes. We dove down under our aunts to make them scream, and then we swam far out where the others couldn't follow us so as to be alone and dive and kiss under the water, which is a lovely way of kissing. Then we all sat on the beach and took turns covering each other with sand, and our aunts and everyone looked at Gunhild's new breasts, but no one mentioned them. It was terribly hot. We swam some more, and then we had to go back and help weed the strawberry beds. When Anna and I were walking back to the house, we saw that the window of that little room beside the kitchen was open. We climbed in through it, and there was Karna making the bed with clean sheets. Anna said, "Oh, smell a bit! Doesn't it smell just like the Milk Inspector?" Well, it did—it smelled sour milk and hair tonic. The windows are only opened twice a year when he comes to inspect the cows for tuberculosis, so it's no wonder that his smell stays on in that room from one year to the next. Karna giggled and said, "The Inspector's coming in just an hour. My!" She giggled some more and put her hand over her mouth, which is supposed to be terrible manners, but Karna spends so much of her time with the cows that no wonder she has no manners at all. She had an elegant glass ring on, in the shape of a red heart, because she loves the Milk Inspector. Oh, we were pleased! It's so lovely when he comes each year with his guitar and sings love songs. Anna said that we'd go and pick some flowers for his room, but Karna told her, "Flowers are nothing for a gentleman like the Inspector. Why, the

ditches are chock-full of flowers now! They don't
cost anything. And there aren't flowers anywhere
half as pink as these I bought for him last year." She
began dusting off the wax ones standing on the bed-
side table in a vase, and it's true, they were terribly
pink. Karna took a cake of soap from her pocket. It
was pink too, and it certainly smelled strong. I
smelled it, and it made me sneeze. Karna said, "I
bought this at the store this morning. The Inspector
has such refined tastes for things like that. You can't
think what a particular man the Inspector is." Later
we climbed out the window and hurried to the strawberry patch. Frida was still pulling up weeds. I said
to her, "Frida, isn't it funny that the Milk Inspector
should care for Karna, who has the manners of a
cow, and looks like one?" She answered, "He
wouldn't even talk to her if she didn't pour so much
love mixture into his coffee. It's a wonder he can
swallow it at all." I asked, "What is love mixture?"
Frida answered, "It's what Sven cooks up for his
rabbits to make them breed quickly. It's meant for
rabbits, but that fool, Karna, gives it to her Milk
Inspector. And she gives him her savings too. If the
love mixture doesn't work, then the savings do." I
heard a noise and looked around, and there was the
Inspector himself marching right by us with his bag
and his guitar, with Karlson walking behind him, oh
so carefully, with the tray with all the little test
tubes half full of milk. The Inspector was terribly
elegant. He had checked trousers and leather leg-

gings and a green velvet cap. He bowed right from the waist and said, "Fröken Jezza. Fröken Anna." At dinner Karna served, and she had the red ring in the shape of a heart on her finger. Once when she was out of the room, Uncle Rolf said, "What's the matter with the girl anyway? Why does she keep on giggling?" Aunt Helga said, "Oh, it's the Milk Inspector!" They all laughed. Uncle Rolf said, "Summertime and the Milk Inspector! What more could any woman ask?" We gobbled our food up quickly and ran out. The Milk Inspector was already tuning up his guitar. He began to play, "Beautiful Northland, star amongst countries!" He sat on the window sill of his room, with his long legs hanging out. Such thin, thin legs he has! Later Gunhild came out, and Gudrun and Fru Karlson and Fru Boberg came from the cow shed, and Frida and Karna from the kitchen. We all sat on the warm green grass. He sang, "The beauty of your body makes perfect my love." That's a darling song, it's Anna's favorite, and then he sang the sad one that goes, "Mother, Father, I am sick, Lay me in the coffin quick. Deck me with ribbons yellow and gold, Make me comely, though I am stiff and cold." When he sang, "I will thee wed," we all looked at Karna, as we do each year. She'd be hurt if we didn't, though she knows very well the Inspector can't marry her, seeing that he's like a gentleman, though not a real gentleman, of course. She clapped her red hand to her mouth and giggled and was so happy. The moon came out, round and shining, which is just what the Milk Inspector likes. He stared at it terribly hard and sighed, and the strings of his guitar seemed to quiver all by themselves. His nails are long, long, and black as black. I suppose that Karna hadn't given him her fine pink soap yet. She'll probably wait till they are alone and she can kiss him. He began to sing, "Moon, moon, far-off wanderer!" Big whiffs of lilac smell came from the lovely bush at the corner. I said, "Oh, how I long for love! Don't you long for love, Anna?" And Anna answered me, "Oh yes, I do, I do!"

34
Anna's Story

When I woke up the sun was spilling itself into my face, and I opened one eye and it got filled with sun right up to the brim. I saw that Jezza wasn't in her bed. She was standing by the mirror, tying that huge red ribbon that used to belong to Auntie Ninna in her hair. It fitted right above her big square bang, which is so fair it is almost white. I said, "You look funny, standing there with no clothes on. You're as tall and thin as a peony, and that red bow is like a peony head. Why are you up so terribly early?" Jezza answered, "MIDSUMMER! That's why I'm up and trying out the hair ribbon that I'm going to wear tonight. The sun's going to be tired tomorrow after staying up twenty-four hours today." Oh, it was really Midsummer Eve! I jumped up from bed, and we ran about the room and we sang songs and were awfully gay and happy. All the aunts have

come home to Berg for the summer, and Aunt Helga
called up to us from the yard, "We're off to the
meadow. Aren't you two coming?" We didn't wash,
we didn't even button ourselves up properly, but
ran out of the house right through the dining room,
where Uncle Rolf was sitting eating his six piping-
hot eggs, which he needs every morning after sleeping so long. He laughed and waved to us with his
spoon. We were almost the first ones in the meadow—
only Thyra and her family were there before us.
But soon others began to arrive. In about an hour all
the women in the village were there, busy cutting
branches and cornflowers and poppies and other
flowers for the Maypole. Karna and Gudrun came,
dragging between them a clothes basket full of peonies, Grandmother's gift to the pole. Our peonies are
the biggest in all Berg, and every year we cut a
whole basketful to make the pole more beautiful.
It was terribly hot. Everyone sweated, working away
weaving flowers into garlands to cover every inch of
that long Maypole. At noon, just as we were finish-
ing, we saw the men coming toward us across the top
of the hill. "Here they come!" cried everyone. Some
of the men must have begun their serious Midsummer drinking. They were awfully gay and kept pushing each other into the hay and grabbing off each
other's caps for fun. Thyra's mother made a sign
to them that we and our aunts were there, and they
tried to stiffen up a bit. They came and said how-
do-you-do, and they kept looking up at the sun,

which was as yellow as butter. Aunt Helga said, "Well, what do you say to this for real Midsummer weather?" That made them loosen up, and they began to fool about again, and even Karlson, who's usually so serious, got pushed into the hay. "Ready?" they called. "All women stand aside!" They spat in their hands and pulled up their sleeves and took hold of the Maypole, which was lying in the grass, green and fat with garlands, with all the peonies and poppies and cornflowers stuck on it. "One, two, three!" they cried. "Up she goes!" Everyone shouted, "Hurrah! Hurrah! Oh, isn't she a beauty!" "Now we must go home," said Aunt Helga. "Children, come along!" We said good-bye, and Thyra asked, "Are you going to be here at seven? What are you going to have on?" "A fine red hair ribbon," said Jezza. "What are you?" "Oh, my pink dress, of course," said Thyra, making a "Friday Thyra" face as if it were stupid of us not to know. But on the way home Aunt Emilia, the Field Marshal, said, "Jezza, you know very well that we can't go to the Midsummer dance this year. We're in mourning." "Not go to the dance!" shouted Jezza. "But it won't be Midsummer Night again for a whole year, will it? Not till next summer!" "Of course it won't," Aunt Emilia said. "You do say stupid things!" Jezza and I let the others walk ahead, and Jezza said to me, "Can she really mean it? Why on earth can't we go to the dance tonight?" "Because we have to be sad about Auntie Ninna," I answered. Jezza got as mad as if a bee had stung her. "What has that to do with it?" she said. "Who is it that's really sad about Auntie Ninna, please tell me that? I mean *really* sad. It's me. Why, they don't even know what it is to be sad! They don't know anything. They didn't know how to love her when they had her, but were so awful to her that she didn't want to live. That's all grown-up people know, how to be awful to one another. Perhaps that's why they dress themselves in black when someone dies, just because they're so ashamed of what they've done to him. They hang black stuff right over their faces so that no one can see their mean, wicked eyes. But I made Auntie Ninna happy! She told me so. I knew how to make her laugh, and I loved her and petted her and never stopped adoring her one minute all my life. And I sang to her and told her funny riddles, and helped her make herself pretty, which is what she liked best. So I have nothing to be ashamed of, but they have." "Yes," I said, "they thought they could be awful to her, but now that she's dead they put on black veils." Jezza said, "When Auntie Ninna died I had such an ache that I got all stiff from being so sad. Well, that was then, but now I feel gay and hoppy about tonight, and they have to tell me it's wrong! They never understand anything. Everything that's right they call wrong, and what's wrong they call right. They muddle up everything in the world." "Well, it's not muddly when I'm alone," I said, "and that's how I like to be. Nothing ever

seems muddly when I'm alone." "Yes, only I hate
to be alone," said Jezza. "I am going to be with
heaps and heaps of people always, but I'm never
going to do as they tell me to. When I do what I
feel, I'm sure it's right, and what I feel like doing
tonight is to dance." "Well, you ought to do it then,"
I said. "Yes," said Jezza. "The sun is going to be
up all night, and that means it is a special night,
doesn't it? If even the sun acts differently, then it
must be a very special night. Everyone in Berg has
been longing for tonight for a whole year, and I
have longed more than anyone, for I always long for
everything more than anyone. Isn't it right then that
I should go?" "It is right," I said, and Jezza said,
"It is right, and I am going. They'll all be furious,
but they can't do more than talk, which they keep on
doing anyway, and I'll have had the fun, and the
cakes and the coffee, even if I get punished afterwards. So I'm going. Are you coming along?"
"Don't be a donkey," I answered. "Of course I'm
coming along." At dinner that night the table wasn't
decorated as much as on other Midsummer Nights,
and the aunts were in black and hadn't made themselves elegant at all, even though Doctor Borger
had been invited. Ever since Auntie Ninna died
they've stopped laughing as they used to, and their
mouths are just like sour berries most of the time.
In the middle of the meal, Jezza began to giggle
about something, and Aunt Emilia said, "Jezza!"
and raised her eyebrows in Doctor Borger's direction.

That meant even Jezza and I shouldn't laugh when he was there, for as Doctor Borger was Auntie Ninna's fiancé, he's expected to be even sadder than the others. But Jezza looked at Doctor Borger and she said, "Why shouldn't I laugh? Uncle Harald doesn't mind my laughing, do you, Uncle Harald?" Oh, he looked happy! It was the first time I'd seen him look a little bit glad since Auntie Ninna got away from him by dying, and I know that Jezza called him "Uncle Harald" just to make him feel that Auntie Ninna really had belonged to him and had been his own girl. That made him happier than all the stupid things our aunts had been telling him to console him. Grown-up people only talk and talk, and that makes nobody any happier, but Jezza looks at people, and then she knows just what it is they want to hear more than anything else on earth. Doctor Borger wanted most of all to hear that lovely Auntie Ninna really had been his sweetheart. After dinner, as soon as we could, Jezza and I got up and ran away. They asked us, "Where are you off to?" and Jezza answered, "Just off!" We slipped upstairs and got elegant, and then we ran to the meadow. Everyone was there, and the two fiddlers were playing away, all drunk and awfully sweet. They were Herr Boberg, our Fru Boberg's husband, and Jon Bolin, the blacksmith. We got some coffee cakes and went to eat them right near the fiddlers, so as to hear the music really loud. Jon said, "Fröken Anna is as pretty as a bouquet of flowers. Eh, Bo-

berg?" Boberg pulled out his harmonica so that it
made a long sad sound. He stared and stared at me
and then he began to smile. "She's a darling! Oh,
she is a real darling!" he said. "It's right that they
should call her the flower of Berg, but they're going
to pick her soon and plant her elsewhere, I'll wager.
I've never known beauty to be left alone." He took
a long pull at his schnapps bottle and sighed and
wiped his mouth and took another pull. Boberg fin-
ishes a whole bottle like nothing. I was sad because
of what he'd said. It's awful the way they all talk
about my being beautiful as soon as they see me, and
about my leaving Berg. I am never going to leave
here! I am going to marry Uncle Rolf and stay on
in Berg forever. Jezza and I began to dance. "Look
at Fröken Jezza!" called Jon. "She's as gay as my
fiddle. Just look at her crazy feet!" Jezza whirled us
around and around, and it was lovely. Later I danced
with Karna and with Karlson and with Thyra, but
mostly with Jezza, of course. At last the long dance
began, around the pole. Oh, how we laughed! We
sang loud, loud, and laughed and danced. Frida
had helped Sven clean the dung off and brush up a
bit. She came holding him by the hand, and he had
brought his fiddle along. He acted as shy as a little
boy, though he is forty years old, but the other fiddlers made room for him and changed the tune they
were playing to one of those three he knows. That
was lovely of them. Oh, Sven was pleased! He
played so that our feet flew. "What's the time,
Sven?" Jezza shouted to him as she danced past,

just as Frida has taught us to ask each time we see him, so he can take out his father's watch. He called back, "There isn't any time tonight, Fröken Jezza!" "Oh, bravo, Sven! Bravo!" everybody cried. "That's right, there's no time tonight!" When the long dance ended we were so sweaty that we looked as if we'd come out of the lake, and we couldn't stop laughing. Jezza and I went and sat in the ditch, but the ditch was full of people already, and everyone was kissing and squeezing each other. Their best clothes were getting crumpled, but nobody cared. Of course we had nobody to squeeze, so we squeezed each other. Karna and the Milk Inspector ran off into the bushes, and a lot of others did, too. I suppose they wanted to kiss terribly in there. We heard them laughing and giggling. When Jon took up his fiddle and began to play, they all came running back, and lots of girls had green on the backs of their dresses from the grass, and everyone laughed at that. It was midnight, but as light as in the daytime, and the sun just shone and shone, and the red flowers on the Maypole were breathing hard as if they, too, were excited about it's being Midsummer Night. Jezza said, "I feel all good and kind because I'm so happy. It certainly must be right to feel like that." She squeezed me terribly and said, "Wasn't it good that we came out here tonight, Anna? We must always do what we feel like doing, and then everything will turn out well. It wasn't wrong, as they said it was, it was right." And I answered, "It was right."